I AM WOMAN

I AM WOMAN

Restore. Inspire. Stand With. Empower Her

VERLISA WEARING   DR. MONIQUE LATRICE

DR. SHIRLEY BOYKINS-BRYANT   TANYA L. HOLLAND

ZANETTA HOWARD   SANDRA E. JACKSON

CHRISTINE JAMES   SHAYLA UNIK   DEBORAH JUNIPER-FRYE

DR. JENNOA GRAHAM   COLLEEN WILLIAMS-RENNIE

FRANCINE HOUSTON   BELINDA STROTHER

DR. ANITA GREEN   KIMBERLY BABERS

TRACEY ELLIS-CARTER   LISA MIDDLEBROOKS

JOYCE JENNINGS

Foreword by
PASTOR MARILYN FENDERSON

It Is Written Publishing, LLC

Presented by: Verlisa Wearing

Cover Design: Verlisa Wearing

Women Illustrations: Canva

For copyright permission contact:

Verlisa Wearing at verlisawearing@itiswrittenpublishing.net

Library of Congress Cataloging-in-Publication Data

Ebook ISBN: 978-1-956075-13-7

ISBN: 978-1-956075-14-4

Published in the United States by

It Is Written Publishing, LLC

Atlanta, GA 30213

www.itiswrittenpublishing.net

I AM WOMAN

DEDICATION

To every woman who has a desire to share their voice yet, are held captive to the unknown.
May you gain the courage and strength needed to take the necessary steps in making your dreams come true.
Your greatest first version of yourself is awaiting your arrival!

CONTENTS

Foreword   xiii

Introduction   xv

Poem of Affirmations   xix

1. BREAK FREE OF FEAR AND RISE   1
Monique LaTrice

2. I AM WOMAN   10
Dr. Shirley Boykins-Bryant

3. I WOKE UP LIKE THIS   18
Tanya L. Holland

4. I WAS CALLED TO BE HURT   28
Zanetta Howard

5. YOU ARE FULLY EQUIPPED TO SURVIVE   38
Sandra E. Jackson

6. WORTHY OF M.E.   48
Christine James

7. LUSTING WITH LOVE   58
Shayla Unik

8. THE EVOLVED WOMAN   68
Deborah Juniper-Frye

9. SINGLE PARENTING WHILE IN SCHOOL - BEST
PRACTICES   76
Dr. Jennoa Graham

10. TIME TO TAKE A STAND   86
Colleen Williams Rennie

11. TOUCHING THE HEM OF JESUS' GARMENT   94
Francine Houston

12. WHO DO YOU THINK YOU ARE?   104
Belinda Strother

13. ADJUSTING TO LIFE'S CIRCUMSTANCES   114
Dr. Anita Green

14. I AM RESILIENT, I AM WOMAN   124
Kimberly Babers

15. RESTORATION - PREPARATION + TIMING   134
Tracey Ellis-Carter

16. WHAT I GLEANED FROM GLO   144
    Lisa Middlebrooks

17. LESSONS ALONG THE JOURNEY   152
    Joyce Jennings

Woman   163
30 Daily Positive Affirmations   165
Resources for Women   169
Thank You   171
Meet The Authors   175
Verlisa Wearing   177
Dr. Monique LaTrice   179
Dr. Shirley Boykins Bryant   181
Tanya L. Holland   183
Zanetta Howard   185
Sandra E. Jackson   187
Christine James   189
Shayla Unik   191
Deborah Juniper-Frye   193
Dr. Jennoa Graham   195
Colleen Williams-Rennie   197
Francine Houston   199
Belinda Strother   201
Dr. Anita Green   203
Kimberly Babers   205
Tracey Ellis-Carter   207
Lisa Middlebrooks   209
Joyce Jennings   211
Acknowledgments   213
Notes   215
I AM WOMAN Extra!   217

FOREWORD

The title *I Am Woman* is a clarion call that delivers a mandate for all women to sound the trumpet and be loud, bold and clear about who they are. It serves as a form of poetic justice because it speaks to your spirit and brings into harmony your heart, mind and soul. It is an affirmation for women to come out of the shadows and take your rightful place in society to become global influencers and world changers.

The Visionary Elder Verlisa Wearing encompasses every aspect of *I Am Woman* because she calls out those who are victims of identity theft and have yet to discover their ordained purpose in life. Nevertheless, the call doesn't stop there, her influence and global reach is notably extended to those who are multifaceted, multicultural, and multi-talented to empower them to reach their highest level of greatness.

Reading this book will help you to uncover who you are and recover your identify so you can change the trajectory of your life. You are woman!! Allow this dynamic book to saturate your spirit so those words can resonate in your soul. You are called to be leaders, visionaries, business owners and most importantly you are children of the highest God, therefore you are already winning.

Once you have read this dynamic book you will soon come into the knowledge of understanding who God has ordained you to be. You will be fully equipped to use your tools and testimonies to inspire others to come out of their circumstances and walk in the power and authority of who God has called them to be.

With great expectations,
Pastor Marilyn Fenderson
One Flesh Worldwide Ministries

I am Woman

INTRODUCTION

I sit here asking myself this question, *"when did you lose your identity? When did you allow your voice to be muted?"* Wow, I say as this is mind-blowing. Have you ever honestly asked yourself these questions?

Unbeknownst to me, my voice was silenced at thirteen in my English class when my teacher, Mrs. Adams advised me to look up the meaning of the word, *loquacious,* which means *very talkative.* I feel she did not intend to silence me in life yet, as you see forty plus years later, I still see vividly her standing over my desk telling me, this I need you not to be, just be quiet.

How many can relate to this? Your story may not be the same yet, you were told to be quiet and as you grew and progressed along in life you began not speaking on your behalf because people did not want to listen, others took your opinions as having a take-over-spirit, or you heard, oh, you think you know everything. So, you now only share your truth, sharing your nuggets of wisdom only to a select few. Maybe your voice is not used for yourself but, it is used to shine for others...you know what I mean, you are the catalyst putting every piece of the puzzle together in the background, creating events, writing the letters, negotiating contracts and so forth. Today, I call you out to no longer silence your voice for yourself but to allow your voice to be shared and heard. There are so many women, girls, boys and men needing to hear what is housed within you. Sis, these people are awaiting their release but, they cannot move forward because you haven't opened your mouth. Speak sis, speak!

Who are you, who are you really? This question when asked firmly and intentional will cause a person to stop dead in their tracks. This journey called life has a way of causing one to wander off in becoming someone they were never created to be. Whether it was in your youth, you trying to fit in with others, when honestly, truth be told, those who you were emulating desired to have the life you were privileged to live. Or as an adult, you played along to get-along and now you find yourself in a place of contemplation of whether you want to be who you are and where you are. Today, I call you out of the dis-ease of not being true to yourself. Today, I call you out of the falsehood of being held captive and call you to be freed...free yourself and be the greatest first version of yourself.

It is a joy to have you here with me this day as we travel down this journey of, *I AM WOMAN*. Are you ready to be *Restored, Inspired*, have someone to *Stand with* and *Empower* you? Within the pages to follow you will be introduced to seventeen women who desire to see you WIN, no matter your current and/or past circumstance or situation. You are here for a reason. Yes, you are reading this book because there is greatness within you and it is time to share your voice, and your story.

After each chapter are two activities for you to participate in, *Dear Me*, where you will write a letter to yourself based on how you feel after reading the chapter. The second is *My Ideas & Inspiration*, where you will write out your dreams, desires, and ideas flowing through your mind and jumping in your spirit as you were reading the chapter. These are actions that need to be taken, dreams that need to be birthed. At the conclusion of reading the entire book, you will revisit your Letter to Self, pondering on where you are and what you changed and/or implemented. You will then, visit those actions written down and will mark off those items completed and place the completion date and for those items not done, you will create a strategic plan to make them happen. At the end of the book, you will find resources that will offer further assistance for what you may be interested in and will provide help in certain crisis you may deal with.

Sis, you may not control all the events that may have happened to you but, you can decide not to be reduced by them and help someone else along the way. Stand and be the *I AM WOMAN* you were created to be. Those scars and wounds received are embellishments of jewels that are placed in your crown. Pick up your crown, put it on your head and move forward in life knowing that you are important and that which is within you is important. Use your voice, talents, gifts and story to help change the trajectory of someones life, they are waiting for you to awaken into your greatness so they may then recognize theirs.

You are WOMAN, for I AM WOMAN!
I Love You Sis Always,
Verlisa

POEM OF AFFIRMATIONS

Monique LaTrice

I am a winning woman,
Favor finds me.
Every seed I sow prospers,
I live abundantly.
My words hold power,
I speak boldly.
I'm on the way up,
I rise gracefully.
Nothing can stop me,
I walk boldly.
I am called by God,
So, there is room for me.

Chapter One

BREAK FREE OF FEAR AND RISE

Monique LaTrice

I've always thought I was comfortable in my skin, but now as a woman coming into her own I must admit that wasn't true. I'm just now becoming comfortable and confident at this stage in my life. A lot of what was holding me back when I was younger was fear, comparison, and self-doubt. One thing I had to get over was saying no to things I wanted to do because I was afraid, I might fail, afraid of being outside my comfort zone, and afraid of what others would think. I allowed fear to prevent me from speaking up for what I wanted, pursuing dreams, and fully living. Fear had a chokehold on me, so much so I figuratively lost my voice as I shrank into the background and rendered myself invisible. Fear has the power to overtake us if we allow it; don't let fear be greater than your faith.

I WANTED TO BE A WRITER. IN FACT, THAT'S WHAT I PLANNED TO DO after I graduated college. After applying to several Grad school's creative writing programs and receiving several rejection letters, I became discouraged and gave up on my dream of writing. I took those rejection letters as a sign I was not supposed to be a writer and made other plans for my life. As I was reading a book one day a colleague noticed the book I was reading and told me she had just read the same book. While we chatted about the author's work I mentioned that I used to write. I will never forget the look on her face when she said, "Used to write?" She seemed excited and asked if she could read something I had written. I agreed and later reluctantly sent her a copy of a short story I had written. The next day she came into my office and said, "Girl, why are you sitting on your gift?" She enjoyed the story I had written and wanted to know what would happen next with my protagonist. I thanked her for the compliment but wrote nothing else until years later.

I DOUBTED MY SKILL AS A WRITER AND WAS CONSTANTLY COMPARING myself to published authors. This was overwhelming to where I had diminished in spirit, voice, and purpose. One day I heard a voice say, "*Let your light shine.*" I ignored it, believing I no longer had any light, and I continued allowing myself to shrink into the background. I was hiding my voice from the world to protect myself from embarrassment without realizing I could never hide from purpose. I had created excuses to not write and allowed comparison to stifle my creativity. There was a plan for my life that did not involve me hiding away and remaining silent. So, I drafted a manuscript authoring my story about the discovery that my Dad was not my birth father. My draft wasn't perfect, but it was the outlet I needed to share and release. Whether anyone would read my draft or not, the words that were too difficult to come out of my mouth had left my head and been put onto paper. Once I let go of fear, I discovered my voice as a writer and saw the purpose behind my words. I had a story to tell, and no matter how many others have had a similar story, my story was unique because it was mine and my words will touch those who are meant to hear what I have to say. Don't let fear, insecurity, or lack of keeping up with others hinder you from doing anything you want to do. Face your fears and you will soar.

EVERYTHING WORTH DOING COMES WITH SOME DISCOMFORT AND A little fear. Here's how I continue to work to overcome this fear, the first step for me was to squash my belief it's not cool to talk about myself. I was afraid that I would be seen as big-headed or self-absorbed, if I spoke up about what I do, what I want to do, and what I've accomplished. Don't worry so much about what other people think, be your own cheerleader. I resist the urge to compare myself to others remembering that everyone has their own journey. Your worth is not determined in comparison to anyone else. I gradually stepped outside of my comfort zone.

2 Timothy 1:7, *"God has not given us the spirit of fear, but of power and of love and of a sound mind."* Repeat it until you believe it!

COMPARISON WILL KEEP YOU STUCK IF YOU LET IT BECAUSE YOU WILL never feel like what you are doing is enough. I find myself at times looking at someone else's journey then questioning am I good enough or am I cut out to be a writer. Asking if I have written enough, if my words even matter, and feeling I should be farther along than I am by now. When we compare ourselves to others we expend unnecessary energy trying to keep up with someone else instead of focusing on moving ourselves forward. You might be feeling the same way, but just remind yourself of how far you have come, and what you have accomplished already and keep moving forward.

Galatians 6:4, *"Each one should test their own actions. Then they can take pride in themselves alone, without comparing themselves to someone else."*

. . .

3

DROWN OUT THE VOICE OF SELF-DOUBT BY SPEAKING UP FOR YOURSELF. It demonstrates that you stand by your beliefs and have the integrity to follow through. Self-advocacy has been key for me in overcoming self-doubt and ultimately becoming more confident. Here are some things to remember which continually help me to show up as my own biggest advocate:

- **Get clear on what you want and need.**

Clarity is the first step towards self-advocacy. You can't go for what you want if you don't know what it is. Make time to regularly check in on where you are and where you want to be. What is working well in your life, and where is there friction? Where should you grow and what is your plan for achieving your goals? Be honest with yourself and shut out the voices telling you what you should be doing. You need to be clear on your desires before you can transform them into action.

- **Be confident and know your worth**

For someone else to support you, you need to back yourself 100%. If you don't believe in yourself, no one else will. Know who you are and walk in your greatness.

- **Speak life and positivity to yourself**

Affirmations are one way to communicate positive thoughts. Write out what you want to say to yourself, read it aloud, and place it where you can see it as a daily reminder.

Philippians 4:13 *"I can do all things through Him who strengthens me."*

When I let go of my fear, I became more comfortable speaking up and coming out from behind the shadows I had allowed myself to fall in. I'm now a strong woman fearless in the pursuit of having what I desire. It has taken some time and many factors define who I am today, but I know it's possible for all women to develop more confidence and to tell the spirit of fear and that voice of self-doubt to flee.

You are Woman, I Am Woman, and We Are:

Wise...Open-Minded...Magnificent...Ageless...Noble

Date _____

Dear Me

_____
_____
_____
_____
_____
_____
_____
_____
_____
_____
_____

                        _____
                        _____
                        _____
                        _____
                        _____
                        _____
                        _____

I Love You Always!

My Ideas & Inspiration

Chapter Two

I AM WOMAN

I do not need a seat at the table; I travel with my own chair.

Dr. Shirley Boykins-Bryant

For many women have done noble things, but I excel at them all (Proverbs 31:29) – I am Woman! I am constantly evolving to become the best version of myself. I am she who has defied the statics placed on a Black women born to a single, 16-year-old uneducated mother. I am she who travels with her own chair and was the first in her family to graduate from college. I am she who is the first in her family to join and retire from the Armed Services. I am she who is a trailblazer in her own right.

. . .

I Am Woman: She who travels with her own chair — Therefore I do not entertain relationships with those for which I am unequally yoked. This allows me the freedom to worship a GOD who loves me beyond measure. I am free to align my beliefs, morals, and values with those that are printed in the WORD of GOD! I am free to seek forgiveness for each day I fall short of being who GOD has destined me to be and get up to start all over again. I am free to believe that as Proverbs 29:11 says, *"GOD has good plans for me, plans to prosper me and give me a good end."*

I Am Woman: She who travels with her own chair — Therefore, I will not sit at tables were my spirituality, integrity and authenticity are in question. I am made in the image of GOD! My father makes no mistakes! I will not be defined by societal norms and faddish. My father says, *I am fearfully and wonderfully made*. Therefore, as I am I AM ENOUGH!

I Am Woman: She who travels with her own chair — Therefore I do not sit at tables where my priorities and boundaries are not respected. I am a mother who values the family unit. I cherish the experience of motherhood and encourages her son to *seek first the Kingdom of GOD and its righteousness and all else will be given*. I am a wife who places the relationship with my husband only second to GOD! I am a GOD fearing, Generational curse breaking Woman, unique and unapologetic when comes to my Spirituality.

I Am Woman: She who travels with her own chair; in doing so, I am she who laughs at her future: 'Proverbs 31:25.' While I appreciate the past and the present, but thinking, feeling, and speaking from my future 's perspective is a beautiful — and fruitful — thing. I walk in my God ordained purpose; therefore, I cannot be present at every table for which I have access. I get to walk forward in the future that I want for myself. And when I speak in the presence of this future, I will bring it to life.

*I **Am** **Woman***: SHE WHO TRAVELS WITH HER OWN CHAIR-THEREFORE, I am not bound to sit in company where I am not welcomed or respected. When I sit at any table, I bring with me a host of strong Black women who survived the many bricks thrown at them throughout time and managed to build a family legacy with them. Because of these women, I am who I am! I bring with me credentials such as a Doctorate Degree in Human and Organizational Psychology, I am a mentor and a coach. I coach young people with developing plans to show up as the best version of themselves.

*I **Am** **Woman***: SHE WHO TRAVELS WITH HER OWN CHAIR -THEREFORE, I only sit at tables where discussions result in improved communities, where the work leads to improvements in socioeconomics and individual freedoms for those who reside there. It is my life's passion to educate, develop and strengthen my community, wherever that may be. My church, my Sorority, my family, friends, and the school in which my son attends. My passion for helping others is extended to various places. Helping others is something I never think about; I just simply do. I do not mind if it takes a lot of time or if someone asks me last minute. Being enthusiastic about serving others helps me to remain conscious of how very blessed I am. My passion drives me to make impactful changes in the community so those around me are healthy and happy. And even though these are only two of the things I am passionate about, the other ones I am just as enthusiastic about because they help me be the better and kinder person I want to be. As we have heard before, *"Passion rebuilds the world for the youth. It makes all things alive and significant."* This was said by Ralph Waldo Emerson. *"When I do good, I feel good; when I do bad, I feel bad. That's my religion."*

*I **Am** **Woman***: SHE WHO TRAVELS WITH HER OWN CHAIR– THEREFORE, I do not sit at tables where the conversations are not encouraging and uplifting. I am my brother's and sister's keeper. When he/she needs someone to talk to, lean on, cry with, or pray with; I will be there for them. I will help when they are down. Being one's, brother's and sister's keeper does not mean you have to be a blood relative; it just means you have compassion and empathy for your fellow man. It means you care enough to put aside the individual "me" for a collective "we." Positivity can go a long way and set the tone for the other aspects in your life. Negativity can function as a plague in your life and take over. Avoid being negative and maintain your hope.

I Am Woman: She who travels with her own chair; Therefore, I will not sit at tables where my heritage, ethnicity, uniqueness, or individuality is in question. I walk confidently in the footsteps of Black women like Harriet Tubman, Sojourner Truth, Rosa Parks, Mary McLeod Bethune, Madam C.J. Walker, and Michelle Obama. I walk tall and Proud as a Black Woman because I stand on the shoulders of those who have worked in the slave house to a Black woman who now serves this Nation in one of the two highest positions in the White House!

I AM WOMAN!...Hear ME ROAR!

Worthy...Optimistic...Magnificent...Accomplished...Noetic

Date _____

Dear Me

_____
_____
_____
_____
_____
_____
_____
_____
_____
_____
_____
_____
_____
_____
_____
_____
_____
_____

I Love You Always!

My Ideas & Inspiration

Chapter Three

I WOKE UP LIKE THIS

Tanya L. Holland

I n the midst of the storm.

Have you ever heard the saying, "I woke up like this?" In one of Beyonce songs, "Flawless," she penned this term. It's used to describe waking up already put together. It's indicative of needing no make-up, no eyelash extensions, no particular clothing, no beautiful hairdo, no exquisite jewelry, no filters. It's waking up armored only with your smile, your confidence, your purpose and zest for life. How did YOU wake up today?

. . .

I WOKE UP LIKE THIS.

This is how I woke up today...sad, confused, anxious, worried, aching and still tired. I'm wide awake in the physical sense, but my soul isn't moving. I'm stagnant, even as my legs carry me to the bathroom for my body's daily morning rituals. I look into the mirror at my eyes that defy the plastered smile I give my son, as I say, "good morning." The sincerity of my words and the lilt in my voice are a disguise to send my baby off to school with a positive vibe. I hug him tightly and lovingly trying to purposefully NOT convey or transfer my energy. In direct defiance of my attempt, he asks if I'm okay. In betrayal of him and myself, I assure him that I'm great, fine, okay or maybe just a wee bit tired. He doesn't realize that the answer keeps changing. He accepts this as truth, because his mom would never lie to him, right? He grabs a pack of Pop-tarts, a bottle of water and disappears out the front door. "Be careful. I love you." I yell at his back. "I will. Love you too, Mom," he replies. "His voice is getting deep," I think as I smirk. It is deeper than all his brothers and even his dad's. He is the youngest; he has the deepest voice. And he is always hungry, with the heartiest appetite. He goes for seconds and thirds at dinnertime and intermittently eats snacks between each of his meals. My mind is wandering now, with thoughts from all over popping in. I am not bothered. It is a most welcome distraction.

I WOKE UP LIKE THIS.

I turn on the morning news. Part of my daily routine is to check for weather and traffic. What will I wear today? Do I need an extra sweater or a pair of tights beneath my pants? Is there some traffic build-up that will sway me toward an alternate route? Before I get my answer, I hear "Breaking News." I hold my breath. *An 18-month-old baby was killed by a ricocheted stray bullet. Nearly 100 more people lost their lives yesterday in the US with Covid-19 related illnesses. An 87-year-old grandmother is pushed to her premature death from a subway platform by a hooded stranger.* I digress, "Is it warm enough to wear a dress?" The anchor ignores my silent question. *The Russians have forced more Ukrainians out of their homes to seek safety. A teenage boy has killed 23 seven-year-olds and 2 teachers at a Texas elementary school. The gas prices have skyrocketed and there is a shortage on baby formula.* I exhale. As an afterthought, the meteorologist calls for thunderstorms and suggest that mass transit is the best option. "Tell that to the innocent, dismembered grandmother," I think to myself. The only good news is that the rain can disguise the tears that have begun to form on my cheeks. All I wanted to know is whether I should pack an umbrella.

I WOKE UP LIKE THIS.

My job is not going well. The people there are zapping my energy. The lack of professionalism and ongoing inconsistencies make for a lackluster environment. Hard workers get rewarded with harder work assignments. Even my own work ethic has been compromised, as I often concentrate on what others are doing or not doing. My aura is off, dulled, not emanating the vibrance that is usually illuminating around me. I have always prided myself in doing my best and being the best, competing with nobody other than myself. I now find myself focusing on being overworked and under-appreciated and it's making me bitter. I can't quit. This is not just a job, but a quite lucrative career. I am on the last leg of the race as my pension summons me to stay the course for another NINE years. I've promoted three times, yet work has become mundane. I've worked at my current job for over 21 years and I've been employed for almost 40 years total. What's another nine, right? Uggghhh!!! So, I shower, dress, pack a few snacks, grab my coat, my pocketbook, my headphones and head out the door. I get half-way down the block and turn back around. I take another five minutes to find my second most misplaced item: my phone. What's in first place you may ask: My keys!!!! I can NEVER find those.

I WOKE UP LIKE THIS.

My entire body is aching. I have stress knots in my shoulders, on my neck and all along my back, and most recently, in my buttocks and legs. The huge masses in my legs have restricted my "normal" walking pattern and have made simple functions, like walking upstairs, a complicated chore. I climb the steps like my three-year-old granddaughter, grabbing the rail tightly and moving slowly, methodically. One step, two step, right foot, left foot, I count as I walk. My granddaughter has the perfect excuse: her legs are pint-sized, she's a toddler. My legs, however, just refuse to cooperate. I get up from the sofa slowly. My deliberate movements are coupled with the groans and grimaces that frequently accompany them. Deep tissue massages, hot Epsom salt baths, acupuncture sessions and light yoga act as only temporary solutions to what has become an increasingly consistent problem.

I WOKE UP LIKE THIS.

The nights are unbearable, as I toss and turn yearning for anything that remotely resembles rest, relaxation and/or sleep. My body desperately wants to press the reset button, but my mind, in direct contrast, won't stop racing. Instant replays of the day's events, the weekly to-do engagements, the monthly bills appear in my head like a black and white television screen. Planning for my chapter in the next book, figuring the price list for my merchandise at the Juneteenth celebration, preparing my seating arrangement for my 50th Birthday Masquerade party all plague me. My mind is racing non-stop, and sleep seems like a beautiful, far-away memory. I contemplate a sleeping pill, but the time on the clock screams out, "Too late, you've missed your window!" The light snores of my husband taunt me. The melodic breathing seems to whisper "peace". I cringe with envy.

I WOKE UP LIKE THIS.

My family unit is breaking down. What I once thought were unbreakable bonds have proven to be filled with bouts of dishonesty, jealousy and back-biting. Brother against brother, mother against child, husband against wife are now the norm. The difference is that now I need not look outside my own circle to witness them. I am a product of familial dysfunction. I have, for far too long, placed "family" on an undeserved pedestal based solely on blood. I have been true to relationships that have chipped away at the very fiber of my existence, just because we are related. Family secrets have been generational, and if you dare leak one, even in truth, you become ostracized. Mistrust and disloyalty have become sacred because they offer safety. I seek the freedom of honesty and rebuke the tales that hold those truths captive. I continue to acknowledge my ancestry, but most of my "family" no longer share my DNA.

I WOKE UP LIKE THIS.

I awake this morning with a song in my heart and a smile on my face. I hum the words to "Better Than Blessed" because I know that troubles don't last always. I awake today with the promises of the Lord and Savior Jesus Christ. I wake up with the Armor of God.

I PLACE ON MY HEAD THE HELMET OF SALVATION:

1 Thessalonians 5:8 *"But let us, who are of the day, be sober, putting on the Breastplate of faith and love; and for a Helmet, the hope of salvation"*

I PLACE ON MY BODY THE BREASTPLATE OF RIGHTEOUSNESS:

Proverbs 4:23 *"Above all else, guard your heart, for everything you do flows from it"*

I HOLD IN FRONT OF ME THE SHIELD OF FAITH:

1 Peter 5:9 *"Resist him, standing firm in the faith, because you know that the family of believers throughout the world is undergoing the same kind of sufferings"*

AROUND MY WAIST, I WEAR THE BELT GIRTED WITH THE TRUTH:

Ephesians 6:14 *"Stand therefore, having your loins girt about the truth, and having on the Breastplate of righteousness"*

IN MY HAND I CARRY THE SWORD OF THE SPIRIT:

Hebrews 4:12 *"For the Word of God is quick and powerful, and sharper than any two-edged sword, piercing even to the dividing asunder of soul and spirit,* *and any of the joints and marrow, and is a discerner of the thoughts and intents of the heart."*

I WALK IN THE SHOES OF THE GOSPEL:
> **Ephesians 6:15** *"And your feet shod with the preparation of the Gospel of Peace."*

AND LAST, I KNEEL IN CONSTANT PRAYER:
> **Ephesians 8** *"Praying always with all prayer and supplication in the Spirit and watching thereunto with all perseverance and supplication for all saints."*

AND I KNOW WITH ALL CERTAINTY THAT...
> "No weapon formed against me will prosper." **Isaiah 54:17**

HOW DID YOU WAKE UP TODAY???

Are you tired, weak, frustrated or frazzled? It is time for you to grab ahold of that strength that permeates through your blood. It is time for you to rely on "The Blood." Sisters, daughters, mothers and friends, this is your time. You carry your worth in your spirit. It is time to move with dignity, to walk with pride, to strut in your purpose, to dance with praise. Regain your power and carry on! Wake up!!! I summon you again my beautiful Queens "How did you wake up today?"

And just in case you didn't know...

I Woke Up Like This...I Am Woman!

Witty
Obliging
Magnetic
Adaptable
Nourishing

Date _____

Dear Me

_____
_____
_____
_____
_____
_____
_____
_____
_____
_____
_____
_____
_____
_____
_____
_____
_____
_____

I Love You Always!

My Ideas & Inspiration

Chapter Four

I WAS CALLED TO BE HURT

Zanetta Howard

S he sits in silence understanding her place. She downplays her talent, gifts, sense of humor, self-worth and overall wellness be it mental, emotionally, or physical.

SO MANY PEOPLE HAS JUDGED HER BASED UPON THEIR PERCEPTION OF her. She is never good enough for them no matter how much she pours out or into them be it spiritual, physical, emotional, mental, or financially.

RISING EARLY HOURS PREPARING FOR THE ONES SHE LOVES NEVER taking thought on what she needs; her focus is on what the husband needs. Her children are young and need attention, but she focuses on the need of her husband, to her she is this called to do!! She does not mind she's excited and feels it's really an honor to prepare her spouse to go out and succeed in his endeavors!!

SHE NOW REALIZES HOWEVER, DOES NOT KNOW WHEN HER ASSISTANCE OF encouragement, sacrifice and joy transitioned from freely given time above and beyond that, time she really didn't have that is now at the center of her marital problems! Remember she is a full- time employee, mother, daughter, sister and so much more. She finds what she loved to do so freely has become the elephant in the room because she is getting too much attention. She is now being accused of trying to be more, trying to lead due to people loving and respecting her and now she has been labeled as trying to take over.

HOWEVER, AS A WIFE IT IS NEVER YOUR INTENTION NOR FOCUS TO take over anything because you rather do what God called you to do and that is to minister to and support your husband; she is just trying to be a child of God, wife and, mother!

WHAT SO MANY FAIL TO REALIZE IN RELATIONSHIPS IS THE INDIVIDUAL you married had a whole life before you and was doing good in their relationship with God and others while working and enjoying life. Many times, relationships, reputation, and stellar character is already established. What attracted you is now used as a yolk!

I am not a victim I am victorious; I am not discouraged; I am an encourager!

For so long people have taken a back seat in relationships! They've looked for the persona of the white picket fence marriage (husband, wife, house, children, and a nice backyard) or because of what they have fashioned in their own minds about marriage!

Let me share a little about me. I dated my husband for a brief period before marrying (in hindsight) wasn't good! We were married for 34 years before walking away. Some might ask the question why did you only date a short time; you did not know him? The only response I can give is you are right, I did not know him, but I was ecstatic over getting to know him.

As I look back, I realize I was carrying so much baggage from childhood to that current time (26 years old)! Unfortunately, I had not dealt with the disappointments in childhood, my feelings of not being enough, not liking what I looked like (so skinny and flat except for the one part of my body I wish I could have hidden, my buttocks).

See, I had my own fairy tale picture of what I thought marriage should be and in hindsight I realized no-one could have measured up to my expectations because it was not a real picture it was fashioned after watching shows on television or snippets of what I observed in marriages from childhood through adulthood.

I always loved church and especially gospel music. At seventeen, I was so committed to being in Church that any other extracurricular activity did not appeal. I was in the Church unexposed to everything but sex (as a teen I thought I was in love later realizing I did not know what love was). I did not drink, cuss, nor party, I did only go to Church!

. . .

MY EXPECTATION WAS TO BE HAPPY EVERY DAY!! THE BEGINNING OF marriage I would make sure I had breakfast on the table, packed great lunches and occasionally have bath drawn and dinner on the table when my husband came home. I thought it was my duty to contribute financially to the household and made sure any sacrifice I had to make I made happily! I am sure you're thinking these were things I was supposed to do, yes but notice between these lines there was no reciprocation. Understanding like I said before I watched these things from television not realizing marriage is a partnership. In hindsight I realize I expected this man I married to be my savior! My baggage was heavy, I shared everything only to later have some of those secrets I shared used against me to justify some of my downfalls and push me into a corner with mental health illness. We were from 2 sides of the spectrum, yes, the Lord was first in our lives, he knew life outside of Church, I didn't.

AS WOMEN WE NURTURE MY NATURE; AS MOST OF YOU I WORKED, cleaned, ran the household, served, and supported in ministry but I did not take care of my own well-being and no one was looking out for my wellbeing! Now in times of sickness he was the best caregiver!

WITH CONSISTENT TEARING DOWN AND STRIPPING DOWN OF MY confidence and character my husband told me that people felt I was stuck up and unapproachable even though I never had a problem communicating with anyone! He did not know on the inside I was always that scared little girl looking out the window anticipating sad things to happen when my dad came home!

HAVE YOU EVER FELT AS A WOMAN YOU MUST MAKE SURE THOSE YOU love succeed even if your dreams are on hold or crushed by non-support?

Remember; Never live your life on what you think you should do or say to please others. I would ask a question and not get a verbal answer however we all know communication is 95% body language! Body language is a strong and sometimes hurtful tool.

. . .

WHAT MADE ME STRONGER IS WHEN I DEPENDED ON MY INTELLECTUAL capabilities! I have been blessed to excel in life even when I was not equipped to do so! This was done through furthering my education in my field, favor of God, on the job training and always paying attention to my surroundings to learn. However, when I did not receive support in these endeavors my mind told me I failed. I can remember major milestones in my life I was to be honored for but I would make excuses not to show up because the support was not there and like I mentioned before body language speaks loudly!!

I'VE MADE SO MANY EXCUSES FOR THE LACK OF MY SUPPORT'S ACTIONS and let it pass topically but on the inside, I was torn up! I learned to live with this by telling myself I had to forgive because it were anyone else on the street I would forgive!

WHILE I WRITE THIS, I REALIZE THAT I WAS A STRONG WOMAN WITH misplaced strength, misplaced need of encouragement! How many can relate to this? It is like being a functioning addict or drunk dealing with my vice but knowing I still had to show up daily to conduct my life!

ALL THAT I HAVE SHARED IN THIS CHAPTER HAS ALLOWED ME NOT TO have any anger or point the finger at the demise of my marriage because I realize I had so many opportunities to stop the mental abuse I caused myself by allowing it to happen! I did not speak up because I did not want confrontation! I told myself/made myself believe it was okay because God was pleased with my dedication and because He was pleased, He would swoop in save my hurts and the day! It does not work like that!

MULTIPLE TIMES I WAS GIVEN THE BLATANT ACCESS TO LEAVE FROM mental and verbal actions showing they had no interest in me; I blamed the devil!! I rebuked the devil and praying to God to cover my marriage with His blood. It is funny now because I can just imagine God looking at me saying look at this mess; the mess was me showing up daily as if nothing were happening, smiling making sure everything looked good not near good!

I PLAYED A PART IN THE NOT GOOD BECAUSE I DID NOT BELIEVE WHAT was in front of me, I did not believe things told. I cut people off including immediate family members for saying damning things against my marriage. I made it so easy for my mate to feel like all was cool because no matter what I would not leave and they could do whatever they wanted do!

BELIEVE ME THIS IS NOT A VICTIM SPEAKING THIS IS TRANSPARENCY speaking! I need you to stand up and acknowledge what is real, do not continue in the same vein but speak up and realize you have the control to decide your destiny! Never dummy down your self-worth, never allow unsought competition between you and your spouse make you feel you are nothing!! ***You are somebody, I am somebody!*** *I am **Woman**, **YOU** are **Woman***!!

I AM THANKFUL I WAS CALLED TO BE HURT SO I MAY HAVE THE courage to share hoping to help someone else. I often asked the Lord throughout my life, "why do I have to go through this, why can't I fight back, why can't I say what I'm thinking?" God why am I such a punk, why am I allowing people to walk over me, why do I have to prove myself, why do those I love think I compete with them, why does it seem everything is just always blah blah blah?

GOD IS SHOWING ME I WAS CALLED TO BE HURT NOT JUST IN MARRIAGE but in relationships period. That may sound crazy to someone however, I can help so many to understand that they are not alone, they are not crazy, there is a remedy before you walk away and most important there is life after hurt!!! The most amazing part is God is so faithful that even in your hurt, your mistakes, all of your challenges God shields you from what could've been.!

I Am Woman!

Winning
Open-minded
Mending
Anchored
Necessary

Date _____

Dear Me

_____
_____
_____
_____
_____
_____
_____
_____
_____
_____
_____
_____
_____
                        _____
                        _____
                        _____
                        _____
                        _____
                        _____

I Love You Always!

My Ideas & Inspiration

Chapter Five

YOU ARE FULLY EQUIPPED TO SURVIVE

Sandra E. Jackson

"The spirit of the Lord has made me, and the breath of the Almighty has given me life." Genesis 2:7

I am the epitome of the very definition of a woman, not because I was born of the female gender persuasion alone; but because I have worked hard to breathe during and through all that God has purposed me to be. I fit the bill of being an adult female; it wasn't even by choice. A female is one whom God has fashioned, designed, and molded. Some have been endowed with birthing another human. Thirteen times, the sperm met my seed and formed a magnificent embryo. Consequently, out of the thirteen, nine babies were created into this cruel world, stood firm, and emerged quickly, making me a Mother. Now, I am not only a woman; I am a full-grown woman who has now birthed four beautiful princes and five gorgeous princesses. That alone is no small feat; it takes a remarkable ability to breathe on point at every juncture of this game called life.

I KNOW THAT I COULDN'T HAVE WALKED IN SUCH LARGE SHOES ALONE. No, it takes a higher power to be who I am. God Almighty reached into my DNA and spoke over my life, preparing me for the journey ahead. When life offered me lemons, I utilized them well and squeezed them precisely, making the best lemonade known to man. Why me? Why not me? God has crafted me with His best-sharpened tools so I can handle anything thrown at me.

PRISCILLA M. RUMPH WAS A PHENOMENAL MOTHER; HER EXAMPLES showed me what grace meant daily. God graced us with the ability to endure hardness as good soldiers, ensuring each test, trial, and tribulation remains bearable.

ONE MAJOR LESSON I LEARNED WAS THAT EVERYONE WOULD NOT TREAT you fair, even though you deserve to be. Please don't allow it to shake or move; you. The quicker it's implemented, the faster your life can be whole.

NEXT, ALWAYS KNOW WHOM YOU ARE IN ANY SITUATION. HAVE IT ingrained in your brain so that when the enemy sticks up his head, you can define yourself by saying, oh, no, not today, devil! "I Am-Woman!"

. . .

THIRD, MY MOM TAUGHT ME TO WALK INTO A CROWDED ROOM WITH my head held high, not afraid or intimidated by the facial expressions or thoughts running rampant in others' brains. Why? Because I am created by the best with the best, and I know who and whose I am. I am brilliant, intellectual, sassy, and everything between. I am happy, courageous, unstoppable, and full of liberty. I didn't create myself. God created me. He took His time and sprinkled me with every spice needed to conquer and win. Now it is up to me to walk and talk the talk. The decision is in my hands.

DEUTERONOMY 28:13 FORCES ME TO ANSWER A FEW QUESTIONS. WILL I be weak and vulnerable? Or will I be a powerful and fearless influencer? Will I be the head and not the tail? Or will I be trapped in a life of disgust and misery without accountability? Will I be above and not beneath? Or will I be the lender and not the borrower? It's all up to me because I have been equipped in advance! The decree from above says, *"The Lord will make you the head and not the tail, and thou shalt be above only, and thou shalt not be beneath; if that thou hearkens unto the commandments of the LORD thy God, which I command thee this day, to observe and to do them."* (KJV) The Spirit of the Lord has made me on purpose for an essential purpose. The breath of the Almighty has given me life for a greater purpose, and I must welcome each person assigned to my life to have the triumphant strength to be all that God has created me to be. *I AM WOMAN* and proud to be!

IT'S ALL RIGHT TO HOLD YOUR HEAD UP HIGH, AND I WILL SHARE WITH you why. As I silence myself, my mind reflects on a dark time when I lived in Riverdale, Illinois. I was a young wife and mother of three children. The level of suffering reached a crescendo, and I had to think outside the box or throw a pity party. I chose to be creative, resilient and think outside the box. We lived in a small pleasant makeshift home where we worked hard putting brand new Empire Carpet on the old wooden floors covering up the years of wear and tear. We fixed the toilet, balanced it, and replaced the old seat with a new one. We upholstered our designer round-bed with a to-die-for rich green covering. We laid down flooring in the laundry room together, bonding and making a house a happy home.

HOWEVER, ONE DAY I WOKE UP TO DARKNESS. THE SUN SHONE slightly through the small windows, but nothing happened when I flipped the light switch. It wasn't because the bulb had extended its last flicker of light, but the electricity bill had not been paid. What can I do in a dark home with three young, robust children? I became creative with my thoughts as I planned our day. I needed to press my hair, bathe each child quickly and take them to the park, allowing them to play on the swings, jungle gym, slide, and walk the plank. I will take them to the library and let them sign out a few books to read. I will then take them to the corner restaurant bidding time, allowing them to order, eat, talk, and relax so when they arrived home, we could sit around in a circle reading bedtime stories causing them to reach a state of exhaustion. To my surprise, we concluded at home in the evening, I read multiple books, and they weren't tired. The more I read, the more they wanted to hear about *Little Red Riding Hood*, *The Three Bears*, and other nursery rhymes. So, I said, "the first person asleep will get a reward when they wake up." They ran to their beds and quickly were out like a light!

RESILIENCE IS WITHIN ALL OF US! BUT HOW DID I PRESS AND CURL MY hair that had shriveled from the humid heat without electricity? My resilient brain stirred. I rushed to the gas station restroom while the children were asleep and curled my hair. The children never picked up on grown folks' affairs. When we are trusted with the heavy stuff, it is vitally important not to crumble and complain but to suit up with extreme creativity.

GROWING UP IN A LOVING NON-SUFFERING HOUSEHOLD WITH fantastic parents and fourteen siblings was a great experience. We lived in a large suburban upstate home in New York with all the bells and whistles; our utilities were always on. I never dreamt in a million years that the turn of events I would endure for 20 years would be so.

41

However, I wouldn't be who I am today had I not suffered and endured like a good soldier. That was the beginning of my suffering years. However, it was not the end. I have been evicted several times, even from major hotel chains. The embarrassment of nine innocent children tagging along as parents tried to figure out what was happening was problematic. In my thoughts was Sandra; how did you allow yourself to reach this low level under the disguise of love? It became difficult to breathe! However, it is not my character to allow anyone to dim my light, not even myself.

I THEN REALIZED THIS LIFESTYLE CREATED FOR ME WAS NOT FOR ME, and nothing would change unless I made a paradigm shift in my thinking. I knew that if I dedicated my time to God in a pure fashion, He would lead me out of this debacle in time. I repeated daily, "Lord, how long will you allow me to suffer like this? I thought I was your baby girl?" My DNA was embedded in knowing, trusting, and believing that God would come to my rescue. When would He deliver me was the question that remained in my cranium?

LACK OF DAILY NUTRITIOUS FOOD, AN UNSTABLE HOME ENVIRONMENT, lack of finances, and lack of a lifestyle I was used to weighed heavily on my mind daily. The innocent, impressionable little ones entrusting me to do something pushed me daily. I just knew that God would bless my husband with great employment, and one day, when we awake from this dream, we will be well taken care of for life. The scripture engraved in my mind endure hardness as a good soldier during my impressionable years, but did it mean I was to be stripped of all I knew?

WELL, THE CHANGE I IMAGINED NEVER CAME. TO MY SURPRISE, HE walked into the house after being gone for six straight months on Dec. 24, 2008, called a meeting with the children, and said I know what I can do, divorce your mother. I am not divorcing you all." He threw two thousand dollars on the polished Avant dining room table and said, let's go Christmas shopping! In March of 2010, I appeared in court to finalize the divorce; he was a no-show. I stood with questions. What will we do? How will we survive? Will we lose the lavish home? Will I be able to afford nine children? Will they turn to the streets? Just when I thought from a different perspective, resilience clicked in. I inhaled and exhaled. *What the enemy meant for evil; God was using for our good.* I went back into the court, stood before the judge as they finalized the documents, and saw my future looking brighter. I envisioned the children making educational decisions, getting their licenses, traveling, making deposits in the bank, moving out of town, writing books, traveling the globe, laughing, and so on. I began saying daily affirmations of wholeness, healing, deliverance, and growth; I had an epiphany. There is life after divorce! God shall sustain and support us for life.

I BEGAN TO DECREE AND DECLARE EVERYTHING I WANTED GOD TO DO for us. I made a vision board, and one by one, I witnessed God change my mind, and then my world changed. My daughter purchased my passport, I traveled to Cancun, Mexico, and worked at a credit union in a state-of-the-art facility, worked and reached the apex of pay; graduated with my bachelor's degree, and my children graduated high school one by one, pursuing their degrees, and others are headed to college.

NEVER STOP MOVING FORWARD; GOD CUSHIONS EVERY STORM. Euroclydon winds blew year in and year out; however, I am here today, letting you know God came through. I am happier now than I have been in 30 years. Change is good!

You are fully equipped to survive because, with God, you can do all things!

I Am Woman!

War Room!
Find a sacred space where you can feel the presence of God daily...
Overflow!
God has 8,810 promises; tap into at least half of them
Manager!
Be a leader; manage yourself and your children with grace.
Affirmation!
Daily affirmations will catapult you to the place God desires for you
to be
Negotiate!
The ability to negotiate is necessary for life. You do not have to pay the
total price for everything; no does not always mean no!

Date _____

Dear Me

_____
_____
_____
_____
_____
_____
_____
_____
_____
_____
_____
_____

_____
_____
_____
_____
_____
_____

I Love You Always!

My Ideas & Inspiration

Chapter Six

WORTHY OF M.E.

My Excellence

Christine James

I'm standing in the kitchen, looking at all these jars and cans. As I reached in to grab the peanut butter, I looked at it, like really looked at it before making sandwiches for my babies. I looked at the other jars and back at the jar of peanut butter. Wow, the power of a label. One can discover a lot about food from the label, it tells what it is, who made it, it even gives suggestions on how to and what to pair with. And it tells you the right amount to use and the nutritional value. But if the label is taken off and a tuna label is placed on peanut butter, it will still be peanut butter. If the label is replaced with a spaghetti sauce label it will still be peanut butter. Even if it is a different brand, it is still the same peanut butter. The content inside doesn't change, the nutritional value doesn't change what's inside the jar. The label is not that powerful. The label cannot penetrate the jar and turn the peanut butter to spaghetti sauce. So, if we know that labels can't change a jar of peanut butter then why are you allowing labels to change your identity?

LABELS AFFECT OUR VALUE AND WORTH. MANY WOMEN DO NOT START or stay in business nor enjoy their life because they sometimes are angry, resentful, bitter, not better. Some women ask these questions: I don't have time for this. Why am I reading this? Is this going work for me? What am I doing with my life? How did I end up back here? There's no reason to try anymore. I have always been like this, so why change now?

"Nothing changes if nothing changes." -John Maxwell

SO HOW DO YOU, WITH YOUR BRILLIANT SELF, GET OUT OF THIS RUT and step in the worthiness of your excellence? It takes one step at a time. Let's go, there are many people, including the future you, who are waiting for you to get this so you can create a business and life you are designed and created to have that can only come through you!

I BELIEVE THE MOST POWERFUL FORCE ON THIS EARTH IS THE POWER OF belief! Believing you are chosen and worthy of a life full of abundance and joy. This is in relationships, with yourself, others, and business.

YOU MUST BELIEVE YOU ARE WORTHY! IT FIRST, MUST BE A THOUGHT. You can't act on a thought or idea you never had. You are worthy of M.E. ...My Excellence. Why? Because it aligns you with His excellence. God does not create junk nor make mistakes, and He didn't start now. He creates with purpose and intent. With this same power inherent in you,

you can create a life and business made with purpose and intent. This is tapping into your excellence.

THE ENEMY IS AFTER YOUR WORTH. HE KNOWS THE RICHES THAT bestow within you, that hidden treasure, that light, that if discovered will transform everything! Wealth and abundant living are within your success. The goal of your success is like Jesus, to Glorify God. He designed it that way so your brilliance will attract others to Him. Others will come out of darkness into the light and live a shame free and guilt free life. They will also believe they are worthy!

WHEN YOU THINK ABOUT AND APPRECIATE YOUR WORTH, YOU ALLOW God to use you in mighty ways, you don't feel alone and you can let go of the former and be open to the new. This has to get into your head first before it can get into your heart then through your hands because your words and hands create the life you desire and your heart has the motivation. The motivation is determined by you. Will you create shame, criticism, and doubt or create excellence and worthiness? If you have shame, and still go after life day after day. You will not get what you want. Its shameless persistence to experience the life you desire.

SECOND, STOP PUTTING YOURSELF IN SITUATIONS AND WITH PEOPLE that are asking you to be less than who you are. You have daily decisions to make. Will you submit to the version and the vision that others have of you that sometimes minimizes your God-given gifts and talents? Or, will you wake up and dare to be who God has called you to be and do? Do not enter into doors of fear and judgment, you are unique and you are more than enough...you are M.E...My Excellence! Do not make the pressure, comments, and unauthorized authority of others in your life, the norm. It's time to break free! It's time to be who you are, grow, commit and be kind to others that are not yet aware of their worthiness and excellence.

. . .

You may think, oh-my-goodness how did Christine know; because I have been there and had to change the direction of my life. But, no one came to save me. I had to make the decision and you are beautiful and bright enough to respect your space (mental and physical) from the toxicity that will continue to poison you and your future. Let's tap into your excellence! When building a foundation, it is wise to step away from others that are not willing to invest in themselves or their families (not that you wouldn't be able to help them or pour into them, there will be a time). For now, get a journal and get clear about the life you want; write it out, don't worry about the how or judge what you are writing.

If you are struggling, feeling stuck or stagnant it may be because you do not believe you are worthy of living an abundant and prosperous life. This means it is time for you to believe in yourself. I had to do this for myself first before I could really believe it true for others. It's important because you cannot build a life that surpasses your mind-set. There's a cap and your thoughts are capping you.

Do you think you're boring? Don't have a gift special enough, or look pretty enough, too old? Need more education even to start? I would like to invite you to stop looking around and look up! Your brain is not beneath you it's on top and closest to God. He wants to lead you.

When you come into the knowledge of your worthiness and excellence you will understand that you don't have to chase anything; no money, no job, no man, no dream. Things that are chased do not want to be caught; Jerry didn't want to be caught by Tom, the road runner by the coyote. You seek. Seek God, His kingdom, His righteousness. This is true transformation. This is how you can run a successful business and have amazing life.

· · ·

ANOTHER IMPORTANT THING TO UNDERSTAND, AS I MENTIONED ABOUT labels, it's the same for titles you give yourself or earned. Yes, that's amazing what you have accomplished. I have met beautifully branded women who were beautifully broke. Don't let those titles hinder you from transformation or charging premium prices for premium experiences. Many women stay at jobs because of the title they earned, it makes them *look* good, but does it make you *feel* good. Titles can be temporary. We all serve, every one of us from janitorial to the CEO. This doesn't make you any less worthy and sure enough doesn't dim your excellence! I understand I've been there, I was tied my worth in my title of becoming a dentist, so when I didn't get in, I was beyond hurt (my belief was, I am finally smart enough to be this, I'll finally look like I have meaning and purpose). I didn't see this until I evaluated why I responded the way after not getting accepted (I had some beliefs in my subconscious). Today, I believe I am worthy either way! I still add value and encourage and help other women joyfully. Even if I made dry chicken (I'd be on a good streak then bam .what is this lol). But with all of the up and downs, I still believe I am worthy in my excellence and so are you, beautiful!!

THE LACK OF UNDERSTANDING THIS PRINCIPLE IS A HINDRANCE TO THE joy filled life and business you desire!

YOU MAY BE CHALLENGED BY THE THOUGHTS," YOU DON'T KNOW what I've done. I deserve a lowly life because I have made so many mistakes". This thinking is condemnation and does not come from God, this thinking is an internal prison! Those sentences you say over and to yourself will be your life sentence. In other words, "that sentence is a sentence." Some of you are giving yourself a 10 year to life sentence from something you did or did not do a decade ago. What law school did you go to and learn that?

WHEN I SEE THINGS THAT SAY," BELIEVE IN YOURSELF" I WONDER.... which self? The one you have deemed unworthy or the one God says you are? Most women do the first and therefore that sentence is a sentence for their life. Challenge the statements you say and choose to believe you are worthy. Yes, I said choose to believe. We have a choice, and no longer submit to the villain we all face named ignorance. If you grew up in an angry and depressed or lack-filled childhood, as many can relate to on some level, you must understand and recognize there was a lack of information therefore no action could have been taking but, now transformation may begin. You are acting now and reading and rereading this book. Because deep down you know you are meant for increase!

THERE IS NO SUBSTITUTE FOR THIS PRINCIPLE OF KNOWING YOU ARE worthy. There's no substitution for clarity, love, worth and action. You are clear on why it's important to be clear. You desire to love yourself. You know you are not designed to chase money, attention and respect. As you step into your new life, you may still make mistakes, give yourself grace. You are now beginning to pivot and change the trajectory of your life and your family's life. Study and learn about yourself, while purposefully acquiring and giving.

INTENTIONALLY ACCEPT M.E. STOP DOING IT "YA' WAY" AND DO IT "Yahweh." A new sentence to affirm your brilliance and walk into the new life you choose *forgive your past self for not being the way you wanted her to be.* Tell yourself, *"I believe I am worthy of my excellence!"*

This day I choose M.E. ... ***I AM WOMAN!***

CHRISTINE JAMES

Wonderful
Open
Magnetic
Abundant
Natural

Date _____

Dear Me

_____
_____
_____
_____
_____
_____
_____
_____
_____
_____
_____
_____
_____
_____
_____
_____
_____

I Love You Always!

My Ideas & Inspiration

Chapter Seven

LUSTING WITH LOVE

Shayla Unik

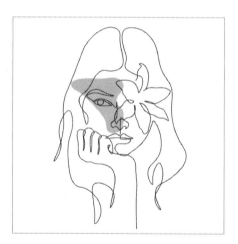

W hen you're a little girl, you watch all the princess movies and read the fairy tales with the 'happily ever after' and envision yourself as a princess who will one day marry a prince and live, 'happily ever after.' I too believed and envisioned this. My favorite was Aladdin. I was Princess Jasmine, and "he" would be my Prince Aladdin (not the homeless Aladdin, hahaha).

. . .

WE HAD BEEN TOGETHER FOR EIGHT YEARS ON AND OFF. HE WAS MY first real love. The one who took my virginity at fourteen. We were from the same place but grew up with a different set of rules. He showed me a different side of life. The wild side. The living fast while you are young side. We always did everything together. Pizza every Friday, rides through the streets and parks. Before Beyoncé' and Jay Z, it was me and him. Everyone admired our relationship. Anything I needed or wanted he made it happen (most of the time). It wasn't just the love or being in-love; we were truly best friends. No matter how much fun we were having, there was always a point where we would take a short break. Not really for a particular reason, we would just take a break which usually only lasted about a month. But no matter how much time we spent a part, we always found our way back to each other. We were forced to go our separate ways in 2003 when I went off to college over 600 miles away but our friendship, our bond....it was still unbreakable. We remained in constant contact after I left. He'd call to check on me often. Many times, he'd send money too. After the tragic and sudden death of his best friend in 2005, I convinced him to move down South with me. He desperately needed a change from the mean streets of our city. He was hesitant at first but a few months later he agreed. Once he arrived, we lived, laughed and loved life! Partying, drinking, road trips, club hopping, more drink-ing, BBQs with a house full of friends, etc. We lived the life in our early 20's! A little over a year after he had moved with me, I became pregnant with our daughter. He was there every step of the way. He knew I was pregnant before I knew. He was there for every doctor's visit, emergency visit and the birth. He was there! Both of us endured the sleepless nights and long mornings. Like I said, we did EVERYTHING together! The one thing he refused to do with me was.... go to church. I was there almost every Sunday. After having our daughter, our daughter was there with me too. Since I was enrolled in college full-time, I would often have study sessions at the house with my friends. Many of our study sessions ended with prayer. We would pray for each other asking God to bless and cover us to pass the test or quiz we were studying for. Although I was far from perfect, I tried to stay surrounded by the people who were exam-ples of the direction I was aiming to stay in. As I continued to attend church and constantly try to push him into going to church with me, I started to see a change in him. Was it him changing or was it me?

Suddenly, his hours at work changed which made it difficult for me to work, go to school and take care of the baby after daycare closed. So, I had to cut back on my work hours which caused money to become tight, and we started to feel what it meant by 'difficult to make ends meet.' One of the biggest arguments, frustrations and separations stem from financial strains in relationships. Our financial strain caused more arguments, and we saw sides of each other that we'd never seen before. Everything between us began to quickly change. I did not know who he was anymore. Although he refused to join me, I constantly tried to turn to the one thing I knew would help, prayer. I felt as though we needed to start praying together and ask God for help. However, because we were not on the same spiritual page my constant request was going unheard. My flesh became frustrated with this. I was confused with not understanding if I was supposed to be leading him to Him or I was supposed to be leaving him for Him? There are so many questions we ask ourselves and so many moments of confusion.

IN THE SUMMER OF 2007, THINGS TOOK A TURN FOR THE WORSE. ALL the built-up anger and frustration we've been experiencing individually and at each other had come to a boil. We got into a physical altercation in front of our daughter. Before I knew it, he was being escorted downtown. I felt as though after our eight-and-a-half-year relationship and two years of living together had all gone down the drain. The fact that we had a beautiful baby girl meant nothing. I couldn't understand how my life had been destroyed all before noon. I was mentally lost, physically devastated and emotions were all over the place. I didn't know what was going. To happen next. What I thought was forever, just ended. Little did I know, this was just the beginning. This was the beginning of a path that will continue to be filled with highs and lows. This was the beginning of my life as a woman. I had to put my fears of failure to the side. Reflect on who I am, whose I am and where I needed to go. Not just for my sake, but for the sake of the little human who called me mom and depended on me for everything life was about to offer (the good and the bad). As the days, months and years went on, life was everything but easy.

· · ·

INITIALLY, LIKE WITH ANY DRASTIC CHANGE, IT WAS A HARD PILL TO swallow. Yet, I had to remember the bible teaches us that couples should be equally yoked. They should be able to pray together, talk about Him and call upon Him, together! If we are not walking in the path that God has created for us, He will destroy everything that is not from Him and a distraction to us. God destroyed my relationship with my daughters' father because we were not living right. We were not taking the steps on the path He created. I had to learn this the hard way. I "loved" this man but, God knew that the love was really a long-lasting lust. Have you ever experienced something similar? What you thought was "true love" in reality, it was a strong lust. Have you ever been at the point in the relationship where you were not sure if you should stay or go? Torn between keeping the family together, and not facing embarrassing questions about "what happened to y'all?".

UNSURE IF YOU SHOULD MOVE ON AND TRY TO TOUGHEN THINGS OUT on your own, even if that means becoming a single-woman/single-parent If you've ever been through this, going through this or someday find yourself in a situation similar to this, follow your heart. Listen to what your heart says. God speaks to your heart. The devil tries to take over your mind. At the end of the day, you get to create the definition of the love you desire and deserve. It's given to us in the Bible displaying God's love. Don't ever mentally beat yourself up! We ALL make mistakes; we ALL make bad decisions. The biggest thing about life is forgiving (yourself included) and the ability to create a new lane, a new opportunity, even a new life! This will even create the opportunity for God to present you with your "true love". The love that was meant to be. It's coming!

LOVE IS WHAT GOD SHOWS US DAILY. UNCONDITIONAL LOVE. NEVER judging, does not hurt and always forgiving. He will give you your heart's desire. What He has for you is greater than what you think you can find on your own.

. . .

LOVE IS PATIENT AND KIND! IF YOU HAVEN'T REALIZED IT YET, THERE IS so much greatness and love ahead for you too. Not because I said so, but because of who you were created by. Because greater is what you're manifesting in your life. The love of the mate may not come when you feel you're ready, but the love for yourself is the greatest and most priceless gift you can give yourself. When you love yourself, you extract a ray of confidence (not cockiness), natural beauty and grace. You keep your head held high to properly balance your crown. When you begin loving yourself the way God loves you, you begin to glow and grow. You're growing through every challenge, every adversity and everything that you thought was meant to destroy you. Even that one relationship, friendship or *situationship* you thought you'd never move past. These things will be addressed and conquered differently. Life is not going to always be perfect, but with love, especially self-love you move differently though those things. You see situations and people through a different lens. The things that once angered you, no longer anger you. The words that used to hurt you, no longer affect you or stay boggled up inside of you mind. Love brings peace. Don't let ANYONE or ANYTHING disturb your peace. You get to create and fully control this space. You get to create and control what your peace looks like. Everything we go through is not meant to hurt us, but for us to learn and know how to maneuver through. We stronger than we think. Even the days or times we don't feel we have the strength to keep going, His love will see us through. This is a part of His promise to us. You and me...WE were made for tough times. We were created to love others but first we must remember to love ourselves. We may bend, but we won't break. I love you; I love me some me, I love the way God continues to shine his light on me. He will continue to shine his light on you too. With love I am confident, I am happy, I am fearless, I am beautifully and wonderfully made...

I AM WOMAN!

Worthy of everything that comes my way.
Openly believing I am the woman I was created to be.
More than a conqueror.
Always looking ahead.
Never ashamed of my past, because it made me who I am today!

Date _____

Dear Me

_____
_____
_____
_____
_____
_____
_____
_____
_____
_____
_____
_____
_____
                    _____
                    _____
                    _____
                    _____
                    _____
                    _____

I Love You Always!

My Ideas & Inspiration

Chapter Eight

THE EVOLVED WOMAN

Knowing How to Lead Authentically

Deborah Juniper-Frye

Evolve - a process of continuous change from a lower, simpler, or worse to a higher, more complex, or better state: GROWTH. *Merriam-Webster Dictionary*

Leader - someone who guides other people. *Merriam-Webster Dictionary*

. . .

Do you know that before you see it, you have to believe it? Before you obtain greatness, you have to work at being great. Believe it or not, those simple concepts took many years for me to understand and walk out. I was that person with passion, purpose, and great skills, but was too afraid to come from behind the shadows. It took this COVID-19 Pandemic and all the trauma-drama that came with it, for me to realize there are so many people who don't carry a title, but have the dormant ability to be an amazing leader - and I'm one of them. You may not have a degree but have worked in a field so many years, that your hands on experience could equate to a master's degree or something of that level. As I look back over my life, it was always my passion and empathy that kept me close to the underdog or less fortunate; and now that has been a foundation, that has led me to lead numerous individuals, groups, and organizations to a better understanding of their circumstance.

According to the Center of Creative Leadership, the characteristics of a good leader are Integrity, Ability to Delegate, Communication, Self-Awareness, Gratitude, Learning Agility, Influence, Empathy, Courage, and Respect. So often, we over judge ourselves and do not grace ourselves with the credit we deserve. Without a doubt, when you compare yourself to others you lose, but when you collaborate and support other women, YOU WIN! There are so many missed opportunities when we are so determined to be a lone wolf, with accolades just for ourselves. However, when you connect to other movers and shakers, it has proven that U-N-I-T-Y is far bigger than an army of one. I have learned that great growth exudes from collaborations and supporting others. For me, I AM WOMAN is much bigger than either of us. Let us look:

W - You are **Wonderfully Made**!
O - You are an **Overcomer**!
M - You are **Marvelous in God's sight**!
A- You are **Anointed for any task**!
N - You will **Never Give Up**!

LOOKING BACK OVER MY LIFE, IT WAS EVIDENT THAT I WAS BORN TO lead and to serve. Being the eighth child in the family (8 meaning - new beginning, hope, bright future), I found myself doing things that none of my other sibling had done. In the process of being cultivated as a leader, it pushed me to read and study about the biblical character Deborah (The Judge), in The Book of Judges, Chapters 4 and 5, NIV. Deborah embraced God's calling; she was chosen to serve at a very challenging time; she was courageous and served with wisdom & knowledge; she supported people; she was trustworthy; she was direct and confident; and was humble to approach. At some point, we all have to accept the fact that we were created to lead. There were so many times when chosen to lead in an area, I flat out said, "NO, I don't want to". But, pushing past my fears I changed to pursue my purpose and passion, which carried me into places to assist the broken hearted as a bridge of hope.

THERE ARE SO MANY TIMES WHEN OUR NERVES AND SELF-ESTEEM MAY have us feeling overwhelmed and out of place, but it's time out for backing down or backing out of accomplishing self-goals. I was sick of procrastination kicking my tail and getting the best of me, so that bully and I rumbled just about every day. What things take you off track? Take a moment to think about it and be intentional to overcome; no matter what it takes. For me, I had to keep daily goals at my fingertips, speak positivity to myself and journal as thoughts came to mind. We must constantly remember to trust the process and gather joy through the journey. *"Everyone wants to live on top of the mountain, but all the happiness and growth occurs while you're climbing it."*—Andy Rooney

I AM WOMAN, LET US DO A QUICK EXERCISE AND THINK ABOUT the things you have already displayed to lead others with positive help. Journal down a few things as you reflect:

1. _____

2. _____

3. _____

4. _____
5. _____
6. _____
7. _____
8. _____

I AM WOMAN; there are so many distractions that keep our head on a swivel looking at everyone else, that we don't pause long enough to see all the good things we are doing. But for me, this year the word "EVOLE" is ringing truer than ever. As the business owner of Grief Care Consulting LLC and a Grief Recovery Method Specialist, I had to clap for myself and say, "You Did That." This has truly been a season of growth for me, as I am confident, for so many of you. What has your past year and accomplishments looked like? For me, it has been full of classes, training, and certifications; it has been saturated with collaborations with other amazing visionaries and exceptional authors; it has been a year of speaking engagements, corporate invitations, and podcasts appearances I want to encourage you to step out fearlessly, casting off all restraints and go for it! There is nothing like collaborating and cheering for other. Start that business, move on your passion and share your greatness with the world. As iron sharpens iron, women should inspire women. And, as you increase in statue and influence, don't forget your declaration - *I AM WOMAN!*

"The pessimist complains about the wind. The optimist expects it to change. The leader adjusts the sails." -John Maxwell

Date _____

Dear Me

_____
_____
_____
_____
_____
_____
_____
_____
_____
_____
_____
_____
_____
_____
_____
_____
_____
_____

I Love You Always!

My Ideas & Inspiration

Chapter Nine

SINGLE PARENTING WHILE IN SCHOOL - BEST PRACTICES

Dr. Jennoa Graham

anaging an academic workload is challenging enough: meeting new teachers, navigating the syllabus, carving out time for homework, and oh those special team projects. As a single parent, it is important to inject and balance these tasks into the everyday chaos that is life. Psalms 90:12 states, *we need to be taught how to number our days so our hearts can apply wisdom* (KJV). As a single mother from high school to graduate school (two doctorates), these four tips helped me stay on top of all things and complete tasks in excellence. The first best practice step of single parenting while in school is to perfect time management in wisdom. Plan your month (yes... I said 30 days) in advanced. Get a full sized 8.5 by 11-inch notebook planner with both calendar style and daily input sections. Stay away from cutesy little purse or pocket planners. These are only good for decoration and are not equipped to hold all the responsibilities God has entrusted to you.

PLAN YOUR DAY FROM THE TIME YOU OPEN YOUR EYES UNTIL THE TIME you close them. Although the unexpected may happen and plans may need to change, having a detailed schedule will help minimize fallout and future conflicts. Have you ever made an appointment or agreed to meet someone at one point in your day only to learn later you have another appointment during that same time? Avoid this headache by having all your personal, children, and professional appointments/events all on one calendar. Here are some other important time management items to include on your schedule:

- Prayer/Mediation
- Cooking/Meal Prep
- Exercise/Personal Maintenance
- Church/Family Fellowship
- Study/Homework
- Dating/Networking Fellowship
- Shopping
- Entertainment
- Commute between Destinations
- Domestic/International Travel

ONCE YOU HAVE YOUR ENTIRE MONTH LAID OUT YOU CAN BEGIN TO plan for each activity. As student, homework and exams must be prioritized over other daily or leisure activities to ensure they are completed. Take your syllabus for each class and place the due dates of each deliverable on the calendar portion of your planner. Do this for every class starting with the first assignment to the final. Then based upon those deadlines, determine what activities are needed to complete these deliverables and place those within the time set aside for Study/Homework. For example, a typical university assignment will require a minimum of 1.5 hours of study time and 30 minutes of homework time to complete.

As a university professor, it is not uncommon for me to assign two homework deliverables per week, per class at the undergraduate level. To maximize financial aid a student must take at least four three credit classes to obtain full time status. For a 12-credit hour class load, eight to 15 hours per week should be dedicated to Study/Homework. Using your partially filled out planner, update the daily section reserved for Study/Homework to record the activities needed to complete homework deliverables. Don't wait until the last minute to work on special/team projects or complexed assignments. Leave yourself enough time before the deadline to review your work for excellence and resolve any technical glitches.

Now that we have the academic portion out of the way, let's talk PARENTING! The second, best practice step of single parenting while in school is to get your children on YOUR schedule. Children are entitled to their emotions and opinions... not their options. As the parent, you set the schedule which sets the boundaries for your children to operate within. As a teen mother recovering from a C-Section delivery, it was important to me to get healed and get back in the classroom to graduate on time with my peers. I took the six weeks of medical leave and developed a daily schedule that trained my infant son to sleep undisturbed through the night. The schedule involved a 5am start to my day and 9pm bath-n-bottle bedtime with preplanned feeding/changing times in between. My hard work paid off as I went back to school, and I received wonderful words of praise from his daycare provider.

No matter how much the activities of your day may change or get rearranged, try to keep your children on the same schedule as much as possible. Children may fight or resist the process, but you are the parent and oversee their very survival. "Children, obey your parents in all things: for this is well pleasing unto the Lord" (Colossians 3:20, KJV). Make sacrifices to ensure all prioritized activities are complete and children's needs are met. I would tell my son in his younger years that if he wanted something, he should want to have a job so he could save up to purchase it himself. He still practices this today as a young responsible adult. "Train up a child in the way he should go: and when he is old, he will not depart from it" (Proverbs, 22:6, KJV). Parenting is not about popularity, social media likes, and personal desires. You are raising the next generation of leaders to care for our future 42 generations.

THE THIRD, BEST PRACTICE STEP OF SINGLE PARENTING WHILE IN school is to know when to be flexible. Yes, life happens, and schedules change however you must know when it is time to take a break. There is a worldly idiom that indicates how dull a man name Jack becomes when he works all the time and doesn't play. I don't know who Jack is or if a nursery rhyme was involved, but there is something rejuvenating about taking a scheduled impromptu getaway. One of my favorite things to do with my son was find one Saturday a month that was free to do as we pleased. I would wait until the night before and review my budget for the month and set a "vacation spending limit." I would then find fun things to do within a 3-hour driving radius. There were national park outings, long hikes with picnics, amusement parks and even random movie theatre adventures. I made sure we tried new cuisines or saw something neither of us ever saw before to make the trip that much more memorable. It's not about the money, although you need to be a good steward of it, it is about bonding and creating memories.

RARELY, THERE WERE DAYS THAT I CALLED A *"DO OVER DAY."* THESE are days where my son woke up in a bad mood and I knew if he went to school, he would just get in trouble, so I saved us both the aggravation and just let him spend the day in bed. I believe today the world calls it a "Metal Health Day." While he slept, I would spend the day cleaning our home or getting ahead on other tasks laid out in my planner. If the

Midwestern weather was nice, gardening was always a favorite pastime. By the end of the day, we were both refreshed and ready to take on the next day with a new attitude. The fourth best practice step of single parenting while in school is to get a good support system. You must have a support system for yourself and a support system for your children. Everyone has their origin story for becoming a single parent however the children should always have representation from the other half of their DNA in their life. Remember, it is not about you anymore, your children are the priority.

THERE ARE THREE CATEGORIES OF SUPPORT AS A SINGLE PARENT IN school that are needed: personal, professional, and academic. Personal support is not a group of people who just agree with you or take your side. This group should consist of family, friends, and loved ones that will be honest with you, hold you accountable, and steer you towards integrity, truth, and excellence. *"He that walketh with wise men shall be wise: but a companion of fools shall be destroyed"* (Proverbs 13:20, KJV). My Spiritual Leader Overseer Thomas A. Pulliam, Sr., and my Heavens Harvest Ministries family hold me to a standard of excellence in God that I am humbled and honored to uphold. Overseer's teaching and preaching has transformed my life and my son's future for the better. Prior to joining Heavens Harvest Ministries, I did have a small circle of friends that did not walk in the way of the Lord however they did support me in truth and love. God pulled me from them and placed me here in Georgia to do his will. I am thankful every day for that transition and look forward to continuing to grow spiritually.

PROFESSIONAL SUPPORT IS EQUALLY AS IMPORTANT. WE RELY ON OUR professional skills to shape the desired standard of living for our families. Wherever you are in your stage of professional development, whether you are just starting out, making a career change, or riding it out until retirement, having a mentor makes a huge difference in your desired outcome. Imagine you have a chest of tools that you have gathered for a journey. You carefully put each piece in its place and balanced the weight so that it is easily carried from one place to another. You are packed, hydrated, and ready to go... but you don't have a destination. Or you may have a destination but are unsure how to get there. A mentor can provide the knowledge, relationships, and opportunities needed to get you to your goal. Without a mentor, you can absolutely forge your own path and accomplish the mission anyway but think of how sweeter the journey would be with wisdom and previous experience as your guide.

HAVING A MENTOR NOT ONLY HELPS YOU MEET YOUR GOALS, BUT IT also teaches you how to mentor others. Once you accomplish what God has instructed for you to do, it is necessary for you to reach back and lift others. You are also showing your children a sense of community and how to function within it. My son has watched me serve as a volunteer parent and board member on many occasions. I was blessed to see him as a high school student teach others music and take a leadership role in sports. Now so many years later, I continue to serve communities and our church in a variety of capacities, and I have the pleasure of witnessing him do the same. Finding a church home and giving our lives over to Christ Jesus, our Lord and Savior was the best decision we ever made. As a Born-Again Believer and university professor, I provide academic support to communities and churches.

ACADEMIC SUPPORT IS ALSO VERY IMPORTANT TO KEEP A BALANCED LIFE support ecosystem. As mentioned previously, there are many challenges in achieving personal goals while maintaining the family structure. Academic support mostly involves staying on course and being accountable to the commitment of education. Don't waste money and time trying to impress others or look good just because you are affiliated with a certain university or cohort. Name dropping is not as impressive if you don't graduate. Education is a privilege and should be taken seriously. Your advisor and/or cheerleading squad should be checking in on you regularly to keep you focused on meeting your goals. The closer you get to completing a course, take time to evaluate how the information learned can be applied outside the classroom. Build a toolkit of notes, methodologies, and key terms that you find useful or interesting.

. . .

ABOVE ALL THINGS, KEEP YOUR MIND ON WHAT GOD HAS FOR YOU AND maintain realistic expectations for pursuit. All voices around you from family to mentors to cohorts must keep you lifted in prayer and spirit. Get negative people and mindsets away from you. Be honest with yourself and your children. If you have a setback, don't punish yourself. Pick yourself up, acknowledge your emotions, and press forward. Achieving God given goals are not just for you; they are for the 42 generations after you. Set a precedence of excellence for yourself and your family to follow. Let God's standards become your standards, through his love, "we are more than conquerors" (Romans 8:37, KJV). Go get your blessing!

Date _____

Dear Me

_____
_____
_____
_____
_____
_____
_____
_____
_____
_____
_____

                        _____
                        _____
                        _____
                        _____
                        _____
                        _____

I Love You Always!

My Ideas & Inspiration

Chapter Ten

TIME TO TAKE A STAND

Colleen Williams Rennie

Dearly beloved we are gathered together in memory of a daughter, sister, mother and a great friend. She leaves behind her children, parents and many loved ones. Taken away from each of us too soon, we hold close to our hearts her strength, love, creativity and humor...is what will be said if you do not take a stand and leave.

. . .

"*No one else wants you; you are not good enough,*" rings loud in your ear. Isolated from those who truly love you and have your best interest, what can you do, what must you do but, stay and try to make it work. That is what they thought. After crying and praying, praying and crying, a phone call is made stating, "*if anything happens to me, just know I love you.*" What dreadful words for someone to hear. What painful words should one have to say.

The eyes of the devil if he has any was seen on this very night. A decision had to be made; would I be separated from my son forever or do I take a stand and run for my life. On this night I decided to change the trajectory of my life and take control. If I died it would be with me fighting to get out of this terrible toxic abusive relationship. This time it would be on my terms! This time it would be different! The buck stops here and this time I WIN!

A sneak peek of my life. The life of a woman blinded by the thought of having a man; that she would risk losing her own life to work 2 jobs while paying all of the bills as she allowed this man to constantly put harmful hands upon her is playing like a movie within my mind only to be brought back to reality of being in a courtroom as the Judge states loudly to my then abuser, "*If I didn't have on this robe I would jump over this desk and hit you myself.*"

This time, this day, the words of the Judge would change my life forever! On the road to recovery, restoration and re-defining who I was and becoming I had to take a long look at myself. No longer could I interact with certain people. I needed to be free so there was no social media, no relationships...I could not afford to stay in captivity with depression being my best friend. See, I had to learn to be my own best friend and to put myself first.

I AM WOMAN...*Woman of Strength and so are YOU!*

WHETHER YOU ARE IN AN ABUSIVE RELATIONSHIP BY THE HANDS OF another or you suffer from self-sabotaging thoughts that are stopping you from being the greatest version of yourself or whatever the situation and circumstance may be; *you are not to fear because God walks daily with you and will keep you from all dangers seen and unseen!*

TODAY CAN BE THE BEGINNING OF YOUR STORY; YOU HAVE TWO choices:

Forget **E**verything and **R**un, or you can **F**ace **E**verything and **R**ise. In actuality you do not have to choose you can do both.

Forgot about everything you had and left, and face everything you are going through and RISE.

Sis, life has more to offer, I had to get that in head. I am special, and God has someone created just for me, I had to believe this! And, guess what? I am now happily married to a man created just for me.

I thought I had lost everything but it is okay to start over. It may take some time to build back up and start things flowing but, I will show up!

Sis, you may have been broken but, God will take what is broken and turn it into a masterpiece.

Change is hard but, it is mandatory!

It's time to make a change. This is the time Face Everything and Rise!

Sis, I see you and I see you have that bounce back!

Today I am a woman rising from the ashes of abuse!

When you want something better you have to make changes in your life, and if it requires shutting down and leaving everyone and everything alone then so be it, even if you have to move away to regroup and start over.

The best part of starting over is, I know whom to take on this journey with me.

You must unlock the story inside of you. Let it be told or else you will fold.

The same story you fear sharing someone is waiting to listen.

I only came this far by His Faith, His Grace, and Mercy.

I am a living witness to the goodness of God. I thank him for never giving up on me.

Even when I turned away from him, He still gave me another chance & I am beyond blessed.

I will continue sharing my testimony. I am not ashamed to tell anyone where I came from and what I've been through.

I pray that my testimony helps set someone free.

Always remember there's strength in every scar, bravery in every breakthrough & courage in every comeback.

It's not about what we went through it's how we overcame it and survived.

Don't ever let your past disrupt your future.

God did it for me I know he can do it for you.

I am back stronger than ever.

It's time to break your silence! It's time to allow your voice to help others waiting for their freedom.

*You can't change the world, but you can make a difference in it.

Every woman has a story to tell. Some of our stories reflect moments in our life we are proud of, some we are not so proud of and we wish we can erase it.

Some of our stories hold the mistakes, failures, pain, and lies that have slowly shut us down or should I say dim our lights in our soul.

Well, ladies, it's time to turn that light back on!

Mahatma Gandhi once said, *"In a gentle way, you can shake the world."* Meaning, **don't underestimate the little things that can make a big difference**.

So, we can start here and start now by shaking the world letting the world know who we are and how it is possible for us to bounce back from anything.

We don't have to feel like we are too broken to be fixed because we are not, we were just made to believe we were.

But this is our moment. This is our time where we dig deep inside ourselves, and look in the mirror and remember who we were before the pain and the abuse, before our past mistakes. This is where we take back our power and our energy once stolen from us before we hit rock bottom, it's time for us to be the women we want to be. Better yet, the women God molded us to be.

Now, is our time, our moment. This is when we stand tall and we fight back! Not with our hands but with our words and our minds.

This is where we say no more, we are not taking any more abuse, disrespect, and whatever else we were settling for.

Remember we are fearfully and wonderfully made!

It's easiest to see better when we turn on the light!

Time to turn on that light let's go!

I AM WOMAN!

Woman, what a strong name it sets me apart from others.

Overcoming all obstacles that has been thrown at me

Mind made up to never give up no matter what

Always remembering "I can do all things through Christ who strengthens me."

No matter what obstacles may come my way, I am Woman that's who I am today.

#Iamwoman

Date _____

Dear Me

_____
_____
_____
_____
_____
_____
_____
_____
_____
_____

_____
_____
_____
_____
_____
_____

I Love You Always!

My Ideas & Inspiration

Chapter Eleven

TOUCHING THE HEM OF JESUS' GARMENT

Francine Houston

A simple visit to the dermatologist changed my life forever.

I was just 17 years old when the symptoms came. It started with a small bald spot in the back of head. My cousin my hair stylist kept an eye on my hair. That was wintertime. By next spring after turning 18, I woke up with a butterfly rash and hair on my pillow. I was in tears. I went to my pediatrician who told me it look like ringworm in my hair and gave me some shampoo which caused my hair to fall out even more. She didn't know what the butterfly rash was so referred me to a dermatologist. When I went to the visit, they took a skin sample and blood test. My dermatologist diagnosed me with lupus. I had no idea what lupus was. That was a disease most people wasn't talking about at all back then.

MY LIFE FELT LIKE IT WAS SLOWLY FALLING APART NOT JUST MY BODY and health. My mother didn't understand lupus or think I was sick. My older sister thought I was in some sin to get sick. My social life was turning upside down. My school counselor thought I was contagious. (Lupus is not contagious. It's an autoimmune disease that can attack any organ of the body).

I FELT LIKE I WISH I HAD SOMEONE WHO UNDERSTOOD ME BESIDES A varsity basketball coach with lupus herself. At least she understood me and helped me out. Looking back, if I could have warned my younger self. I would have written a letter like this:

DEAR YOUNGER FRANCINE AT 18,

I know by now, you just turned 18, and recently came back from the close-up trip in Washington, D.C. However, I know you are sick but it's not unto death. Don't worry about the diagnosis. I know lupus seems like a mystery, but you can live a normal life. Trust me, guys don't hate sick women despite of your boyfriend disappearing after the diagnosis. Don't worry, your sister Tammy will talk back to you. Religious churches think Christians don't go through anything, that's a lie.

FINALLY, YOUR MOTHER, YOU WILL UNDERSTAND AND SUPPORT YOU. You think she's doesn't believe you are sick but she does things will get better. You will live and not die. You are talent and will succeed. Lupus is not a death wish. It will help you get to a healthier lifestyle.

· · ·

I KNOW EVERYTHING SEEMS SCARY NOW WITH THE NEW DIAGNOSIS OF lupus. But get closer to God and increase your faith in Him. Read his Word, especially on healing and believe. Just like the woman with the issue of blood believed if she could just touch the Jesus's hem of his garment she would be healed. You are healed just like she was. It only takes faith of a mustard seed.

TRUST ME, YOU WILL FINISH HIGH SCHOOL AND GO TO COLLEGE. THIS may seem like a rough time but God will smooth out all the rough edges. It's just a test, a test of your faith. God will see you through this. You will encourage others. But first encourage yourself. Despite of what you look like in the morning, wake up and say I'm beautiful.

FROM FRANCINE FROM THE FUTURE/PRESENT

If I would have heard that from someone back when I going through lupus initially, it would have helped out a lot. However, I did have a basketball coach that came by my house during high school and even visited after I graduated and entered college. College was different at least the first year was. I was still trying to stay awake from taking all those mediations. One caused me to swell in my legs and feet to the point of wearing moccasin slippers in the death of winter. I remember having to go to the hospital and take water pills to keep the swelling down. Dietary changes had to made to keep the swelling down. Low sodium diet helped me. From just previously being used to eating about anything I wanted to now having restrictions. I had to learn self-discipline and self-control. Most important self-love because I wanted to live a normal life despite of what I saw others with lupus have.

IT TOOK YEARS BUT I LEARNED HOW TO KEEP THE DISEASE UNDER control until it attack another organ. Every new attack of an organ or body part, I had to learn how to take care of myself and new dietary measures were introduced.

. . .

BY THE TIME I GRADUATED COLLEGE WITH THE ASSOCIATES AND bachelor's degree, I looked like a different person. I lost a lot of weight due to not taking any more prednisone (steroids). I actually felt like I was in remission. At that time of my life, I was still living on my own with my sister who is a year older than me. Times changes and stressful times came. When the stress came, lupus came as well and I found myself back sick again. Eventually my sister and I moved back home and I had to work on my health. My health improved.

LUPUS IS LIKE A ROLLERCOASTER; IT HAS HIGHS AND LOWS. THE HIGHS are when it disappears and everything is back to normal. The lows are when you are in the hospital, can't drive for months or even work. I hit a high at 29 after suffering from seizures and was in remission for 5 years. Then I hit a low at 34 and ended up on dialysis for 5 months from end stage renal disease (lupus nephritis). It was so low; I couldn't drive for months due to high doses of mediation and couldn't work because I was sick. My doctor told me to quit my job because I was that sick. I had to place my total trust in God. Prayer, renal diet, and journal writing took up my time. When I turned 35, two months after I got off dialysis. I thought it would permanently be on dialysis. However, dialysis was temporary.

IT WAS A TYPICAL DAY AT MY JOB. I REMEMBER IT SO CLEARLY. IT WAS MLK day but I still had to work. It seemed so odd. I wasn't feeling sick then. I just remembered doing my job and going home. However, when I woke up the next morning, I received a phone call from my primary doctor about my lab results. They were not good wrongs. She scheduled me to visit a kidney specialist at Genesis hospital. I asked should I go to work today and she told it would not be a good idea. So, I called my job and told them I couldn't come in. My boss at the time wanted to write me up. My mom and my brother told me to stay home and go to the doctor. If I didn't listen to them, I probably would not be alive today. I had to face that I allowed my job to rule my decisions instead of trusting God. So, I didn't go into work that day. The next day I went to the kidney specialist. He asked me to go use the bathroom. When I couldn't go at all, he told me to go to emergency. My sister couldn't take me at that time because she had to go to work so my aunt and uncle came and took me there.

WHEN I GOT TO THE HOSPITAL, THEY GAVE ME TWO BLOOD transfusions. My blood count was at seven. I remember getting an I.V. and the nurses giving me blood transfusions and having several blankets over me because I was so cold. They gave me a room and was trying make me go to the bathroom either or two. I could do neither. My body was filling up with so much fluid. Everyone was praying for me. It was about a few days in the hospital to do an emergency bedside catheter on my neck. They sew it with some plastic thread it was so painful. I just sat in tears then I was rushed to dialysis at the hospital. I was plugged into a machine for several hours. I got another catheter on my shoulder and they removed the one on my neck before I left the hospital. I also received chemotherapy treatment for my kidney. They changed the chemo treatments into cellcept pills instead. I woke up having to take several pain killers. It felt like someone put a boulder on my shoulder. I couldn't use my right arm because of the pain and had to sleep on my back instead of my side. My mom and sister had to help me get dressed for dialysis every morning. I went at 5 am three times a week.

THIS TIME OF MY LIFE, I WAS VERY UNCERTAIN ABOUT EVERYTHING. My future seemed bleak. If I determined my outcome based on this moment, I would be wrong. I had to have faith to believe for change. My younger sister ask me did I want a miracle. I told her yes. Then she said, "Act like the miracle". I just keep thinking about I already defeated lupus in the past and was told by doctors they couldn't find lupus in my blood. Those 5 years of temporary bliss is over and now I am facing a new challenge my kidney nearing shutting down. I signed up for a kidney transplant at the dialysis center however I still had to believe that God can healed my own kidneys.

·   ·   ·

MY FRIENDS FROM COLLEGE DISCOVER MY SITUATION, AND THEY CAME and took me to Chicago with them. I went to my friend's church. It was a week before Easter. That week, they talked about people's testimonies and getting new organs. I sat in service listening to their testimonies and gave me more faith to what I was believing for. Plus, my friends had to me go to the back of the church since I was a first-time visitor and get prayer for my health. They even had food back there. Their prayers help some much.

EVERY DAY WHILE I WAS AT DIALYSIS, I WOULD WRITE ABOUT everything on my mind. I was even journal writing my thoughts down. Journal writing help me plus my dear God letters. I had to go to the bathroom right after dialysis which most people in my condition was not supposed to go. My kidney function was coming back. It was at 10% in January 2015 and by May of that same year it went up enough for me to get off dialysis. I was only one that left the dialysis place not having to do dialysis at home. I was so excited I apply for a job. Most of my family was against it because I was recovering but the job was for people who was sick or had disabilities. I got the job by June 2015 and have been working there since. A year later I moved out of my mom's house and get an apartment again. I thought I would have to live with my parent for years due to my condition however I moved out to see if I could actually take care of myself. I lived with either my older or mom for years, this was the first time, I lived by myself to test if I could make it on my own. I surprised myself, I actually could take care of myself.

NOW IN MY 40'S, I STILL FACE CHALLENGES LIKE HAVING NORMAL blood count and platelets. I am going to a hematologist (blood specialist). He is working on making my blood count and platelets be a normal range. All my doctors are trying to discover why my blood count and platelet count was so low. Some concluded that it's lupus causing my platelets to be low. The good news is my hemoglobin (iron count) is going to a normal range. I just recently discovered that mild cases of thrombo-cytopenia (low platelet count) does not need medication. It was more severe; they would treat with prednisone and intravenous gamma globulin (called IV Ig) are commonly used. Other drugs, such as azathioprine or rituximab, also can help. I am just thankful my case was mild. I still believe God can do the miraculous. By His stripes we were healed.

I AM WOMAN!

We are wonderfully made in God's image
Over comers, overcoming obstacles that come our way
Made in God's image to serve His purpose for our lives
always believing that all things work for our good,
Romans 8:28
Never giving up, but trusting and believing that with God all things are possible, Matthew 19:26

Date _____

Dear Me

_____
_____
_____
_____
_____
_____
_____
_____
_____
_____
_____

_____
_____
_____
_____
_____
_____

I Love You Always!

My Ideas & Inspiration

Chapter Twelve

WHO DO YOU THINK YOU ARE?

Belinda Strother

S it down sis and let me tell you a story. This story tells the tale of a young lady on the verge of becoming! You see, in order to become you must follow a few steps: Think It, See It, Feel It, and Believe It! And it begins like this....

IT WAS THE BEST DAY OF THE BEGINNING OF MY LIFE, I GRADUATED from high school and was on my way to the sun and fun! My mom graciously gifted me with a trip to Bermuda to visit my best friend, Kandra, who was living there at the time. I returned home and discovered that ya girl was knocked up, PG, Preggers, Prego! Being pregnant was both a thrill and a fright as I knew I would be a great mother but what would everyone think? I said what everyone says when young and unexpectedly pregnant, I don't know how this happened! Except, I wasn't lying or stretching the truth, I really didn't know how this could happen because my boyfriend of 4 years couldn't produce children, at least that's what I thought. So, I was pregnant with no idea of what I was going to do other than keep my child!

TELLING MY MOTHER WAS THE LAST THING I WANTED TO DO BUT I also wasn't fond of hiding my pregnancy for long, too much stress. Hmm, I vaguely recall being invited to fly down a flight of stairs, lol, but I know she didn't mean it. I moved in with my nana and grandmother for a few months. I didn't even have to tell my nana. She always said she could discern things about people. Maybe she had a dream about a fish or something? I would spend time between my nana and grandmother's house where I enjoyed lots of yummy food and support. By the fall, I was communicating with my mom again. My family strongly encouraged me to fulfill my original plan to attend college, so I did. It was so exciting being able to pick my courses and I had such high hopes for my future. My heart soared as I pictured myself engulfed in everything ART! I wanted to explore all forms of artistic expression offered. Shall I be a photographer capturing a world-renowned photo in a faraway country? Maybe I'd find myself in the Middle East or Africa digging up ancient artifacts of distant cultures. I could be a journalist searching for the story of the century that would bring me all the accolades and money desired. Maybe I'd get into television production or filming and be the first in my family to make it to Hollywood.

AS MY BELLY GREW, I GAINED THE ATTENTION OF SEVERAL STUDENTS and staff that became friends over the semesters. I was catered to, complimented and enamored because of my dedication to my education. It was time to matriculate, which meant I had to decide upon a major, no more playing around. I had so many interesting choices to make but art was going to be my focus. Sharing my plans with a trusted adult resulted in a slap in the face with her words "You'll never make it as an artist." I believed her! I trusted her opinion and held on tight to her nasty negative words for several years to come.

GOODBYE WORLD-RENOWNED PHOTOGRAPHER! SO LONG TO BEING ONE of the top Black Archeologists! Adios to being the journalist of the century! Salam to being the first in my family to make it big in Hollywood! Hello to second choices, second guessing and a lack of self-confidence. See you later alligator to believing in your dreams coming true because life isn't about dreams, it is about getting things done by any means necessary. Career happiness is not "A Thing!" Snap out of Fairyland and get your head back into reality!!!

REALITY.... WHAT IS MY REALITY? WHO SHOULD I ASK ABOUT MY reality because I obviously don't know what is best for ME! Out of fear of being put down, I kept my opinions, I mean thoughts, I mean aspirations to myself and chose the next best field of study, Psychology. Though, I wasn't terribly disappointed with the field of Psychology and Sociology, it took a few semesters for me to fully engulf myself in my new major. I secretly rebelled by finding ways of incorporating my pure love of art into my projects and papers. Art was my passion, and I was encouraged to leave it behind for what? Why would anyone tell me to leave my joy for something that wouldn't bring me as much happiness and fulfillment? Oh yes, I would be a starving artist singing, dancing and painting in the train station! Insert eye roll here!

ALL MY LIFE I HAD TO FIGHT....TO BE ME! OVER THE YEARS, I wondered if I was good enough to make it as an artist, whatever that means, but fear and self-doubt kept me in my boring lane. It took me 7 years to earn my Bachelor of Arts degree in Psychology because I had children smushed in that time too. I also became a great advocate and counselor for women in the community who had struggles with becoming self-sufficient, but I neglected to practice what I preached. Over the years, I would continue to dream of being immersed in a life full of art: I painted with oils, repurposed recycled items, provided life coaching services and wrote personalized poetry as gifts for family as a way of proving to myself that I was talented. A trusting family hired me to decorate their daughter's room utilizing my recycled art technique and my decorative eye. I impressed myself with the finished product! Fear deterred me from continuing to seek out customers and so I succumbed to a life of banality again.

MY FIGHT FOR LIFE HAS BEEN DESTROYED, CONTAINED, BEATEN OUT OF me! Peter Pan and the gang have moved on because I wasn't allowed to come out and play. Scooby Doo and the gang gave up on me a long time ago! Keep your head down, do your job and take care of your family is all I heard, and I was beginning to believe it!

I WAS 53 YEARS YOUNG WHEN I HAD TO LEARN HOW TO LIVE THROUGH a pandemic? That still doesn't make sense to me but here we are, still wearing masks and trying to make life as normal as possible. It was due to the shut-down of the nation that I was able to stop being whomever I thought I was supposed to be and started slowly becoming ME! It was as if God was telling me, NO, yelling at me to do it and do it now! So, I began to just imagine my dream life with art, success, family, creativity and joy encircling me. I began researching ways to make a living doing what I love and educating myself via YouTube videos, Google and social media. The journey to becoming ME has been scattered with frustration, elation, anger, joy, disparagement, success and a thickening of my skin. I needed to suck it up and stop complaining about who wouldn't help me or who wasn't positive about my choices. I needed to look into my inner soul and pull out what had been hidden for so long. I needed to stretch my imagination, heck, I needed to dust off the skill of using my imagination first. Adults are shunned for being DIFFERENT, for believing in making your dreams a reality, in manifesting things they want in life. Adults are encouraged to get a job that simply pays the bills, provides for the family and ensures a decent retirement package. It doesn't matter whether you find peace, happiness, fulfillment or joy in your career. It doesn't really matter what your name is.... under your job title, lol. I am stating the opposite! I say treasure the difference in people, I gravitate towards those who are deemed socially awkward but are so creative because they have such a great view of life and art. People who are passionate about their art, dreams and living a fulfilled life are happier than those who have just settled in life.

BACK TO GOD YELLING FOR ME TO MAKE MY MOVE TOWARDS BEING A published author. I was scrolling on Facebook and came across an author call for participants in an anthology about childhood trauma entitled, *When I Was a Child*. This call for authors came at the right time as I was ready for the next phase of healing in my life. I was able to kill 2 birds with one stone or fulfill 2 life dreams with one project. Becoming an Amazon best seller was very rewarding, so I signed up to be a contributing author in a 2nd anthology called *Dear Daughter*. In this project I was able to address some issues with my daughter and dedicate my chapter to her. During the time I wasn't writing, I was designing a website for my life coaching business and creating handmade items for my Etsy shop.

IT HAS BEEN A WONDERFULLY FULFILLING YEAR FULL OF UPS AND downs, but I wouldn't be where I am today if not for the struggles. I continue to focus on exposing my whole self to the world in smatterings, lol but I welcome the journey. I recently allowed myself to open a slime shop on Etsy as I fell in love with slime and creating artful concoctions with it, thus the name, *Slime Concoctions*.

AS YOU ARE READING THIS STORY IN 2022, THIS IS MY 4TH contributing author project. If you are at a crossroads in life and you desire to break free like me, I say forget the naysayers and negative nelly's who have given up on their dreams! Find your passion, niche, joy and go for it until you have created your most desired life. I started remembering what my dreams entailed and really paying attention to how the thoughts made me feel. This is how I decided to sell slime as I was absolutely obsessed with it! I carried it with me for stress relief when driving or waiting for appointments. I realized that slime made me joyful and the happiest I had been in a long time. So, be brave my friend and dig deep into your inner soul for what fulfills you. Make purposeful efforts to spend time with YOU doing what WHO DO YOU REALLY YOU THINK YOU ARE?

I AM WOMAN...

Whole in my body, mind and soul
Overdue but occurring in my time
Matter to myself
Abundant and full of love and life
Nova is intelligent, intuitive, fearless and new but never-ending

Date _____

Dear Me

_____
_____
_____
_____
_____
_____
_____
_____
_____
_____
_____
_____
_____
_____
_____
_____
_____

I Love You Always!

My Ideas & Inspiration

Chapter Thirteen

ADJUSTING TO LIFE'S CIRCUMSTANCES

Dr. Anita Green

+**'Justments** (pronounced: *add justments*) is the third studio album by American soul singer-songwriter and producer Bill Withers, released in 1974 by Sussex Records

Life like most precious gifts gives us the responsibility of upkeep. We are given the responsibility of arranging our own spaces to best benefit our survival. We have the choice of believing or not believing in things like God, friendship, marriage, love, lust or any number of simple but complicated things. We will make some mistakes both in judgement and in fact. We will help some situations and hurt some situations. We will help some people and hurt some people and be left to live with it either way. We must then make some adjustments, or as the old people back home would call them, + 'JUSTMENTS[1]

E veryone encounters adjustments at some point in their life. Whether big or small, intentional or unintentional, it's a given we all must go through them. No matter how often and for whatever the reasoning, the adjustments we undergo should bring about a change. Some type of transformation takes place. Before we begin, let us define the word *adjustment*.

According to The Cambridge English Dictionary, *adjustment* means, "a slight change made to something to make it fit, work better or to be more suitable, or the act of making such a change."[2]

BUT FOR ME, AN AFRICAN AMERICAN WOMAN, ADJUSTMENTS ARE adaptations made to maintain homeostasis, which then creates stability and a sense of normalcy. In my opinion, many African American women have made adaptations to survive. I think about countless women who have lost sons and daughters to violence, lost husbands to war abroad and in the streets and have even been pushed to the brink of suffocation when life's circumstances had a chokehold on them. But adjustments produced a sense of a *new normal* just to say we can make it.

In my lifetime, adjustments were made in which I had to undergo changes in my lifestyle; namely emotionally, physically, financially and most of all spiritually.

IT STARTED WHEN I BECAME A PREGNANT, UNWED TWENTY-ONE-YEAR-old. Before I had received my results, I felt like I was another statistic in the African American community. I could foresee the various adjust-ments that I would have to make. Emotionally, I had to prepare myself to share the news with my family. I was navigating myself from shame to fear to excitement to uncertainty. I had no idea how my family or community for that, would receive the news and digest it. Adjustments had to be made. Spiritually, I thought I had failed God, so I had to adjust my spiritual life to make things right with God. Shame, repentance and forgiveness was in order for me. Even in talking with my Pastor, there was to be no shame or guilt. I mean, these church people have known me all my life. Financially, these adjustments also meant that I had to save my money and use it wisely.

But the biggest *adjustment* I had to make was knowing I was on the threshold of adulthood.

THE SECOND ADJUSTMENT I MADE WAS WHEN I MOVED FROM MY hometown Baltimore to Atlanta. Mixed emotions flooded my mind. I left my family, my community, my job, my church and all that was familiar. People were always daily present in my life somehow. I like to say there was noise, movement and comraderies that enveloped my life. Sundays was always the culmination of the livelihood in my life during the week. It was filled with noise, food and people. But, when I came to Atlanta, all of that subsided. Sundays meant no more abundance of noise or laughter, or lots of food nor lots of people. Sundays became my day of adjustments. After church, I had to call my family at the right times so I can hear people laughing, hear the menu and envision plates being fixed as they had gathered around the table. There was the sound of car horns honking and doors slamming. I had an indelible appreciation for noise. After we hung up the phone, I was ecstatic because I had my fix of noise. People and relationships that carried me through my life were no longer there, or at least close by. I had to adjust to developing new friendships and relationships. Instead of being the one whom was comfortable around people, I now had to seek such acquaintances. And throughout my years being in Atlanta, it has worked out. These adjustments helped to change me and my mindset.

THE MOST MAJOR AND TESTING ADJUSTMENT IN MY LIFE OCCURRED DUE to the death of both of my parents. What a major adjustment! I had to adapt to the fact there could be no more random calls day and night, no more visits home to see them. The familiar voices that laughed and sang were now physically silent. It was a big adjustment, one in which I thought I wouldn't survive. The hands of my mother that taught me to cook, the hands belonging to my father that showed me how to change a tire. The voice of reason that belonged to my mother whose soothing voice reminded me that everything will be alright. The tall stature of my father sitting on the side of the bed reading his Bible. These images I would no longer see. Emotional adjustments rendered me weaving in and out of my emotions. Physically I had to adjust to the fact that they would no longer be at the family home to greet me. Spiritually I missed going to church with them. These adjustments caused me to understand that life is fleeting and to cherish each and every moment, whether it be in person or by phone. These adjustments caused me to begin new rituals that borrowed from them and merge with new ones on the horizon. I adapted to the fact that now **I am** now the matriarch. What a daunting adjustment to be made.

ONE THING FOR CERTAIN WILL BE HOW I HAVE HANDLED ADJUSTMENTS in my life. I believe that some may have produced favorable results, while others provided an opportunity to readjust myself and my priorities. When events in one's life occurs, part of the process is determining how the adjustment will be made so it will not have a negative outcome. Balancing priorities and adjusting to the present reality is essential.

SOMETIMES LIFE RENDERS US TO LEARN THAT ADJUSTING PARTS OF OUR life journey is to be made. I mean, aren't we often trying to make improvements? Things may not be where you want them to be, so we adjust things in our life to help us obtain them or to get rid of them.

How do we make adjustments that are intentional? As I contemplated navigating through this journey called life, I reflected on some points.

Number 1: understand and take the time to process the situation at hand in order to develop a plan or a goal.

Number 2: prioritize your plan of action.

Number 3: take your time and remember to do things in your own timing because making adjustments takes time no matter how big or small. There is no need to hastily make a decision that may need to be altered once again.

Number 4: put said plan in motion.

Number 5: once the task is completed, then evaluate to see if your adjusted plan of action was detrimental or productive.

WHENEVER POSSIBLE, WE SHOULD ALLOW OUR ADJUSTMENTS TO TEACH us a lesson. Not all adjustments in life are bad. Some adjustments are made because of life's circumstances and transitions. But whatever the cause, we should want to make sure we are covered. Imagine if you were handed a map to figure out how to get to a new destination. The challenge is that you cannot go the normal route. So, the end result is that you have to map out a plan of action and adjust your route and adjust the timing. Other adjustments will fall into place. What if there was a mother who couldn't afford to buy groceries for her family with what she had. Wouldn't you adjust the price so the money she had she could afford some food? Think about it, what if you were running late for an appointment. Wouldn't you make the necessary adjustments to inform them of your situation and come up with a solution?

YOU KNOW, AS I THINK BACK ON MY ABOVE-MENTIONED SITUATIONS, the necessary adjustments made me stronger. As a single unwed new mother, I had to shift or adjust my mindset to adapt to my new role. Some things I desired to do or places I desired to go I could not do so. Everyday tasks had to be readjusted and my focus was re-shifted.

MY JOURNEY TO ATLANTA HAD TO BE CAREFULLY THOUGHT OUT. EACH day was different as I adjusted my way of living. Even my priorities were changed. I had to think, do and fend for myself. There was no one else around, family or friend able to show me the way.

As I dealt with my grief, I realized that my whole life shifted. Again, I felt alone and had to adjust to the reality that my parents, my lifelines were gone. As I searched and researched for anything to help with my pain, I could find nothing that was suitable enough for me. For I had transitioned from being a daughter, a sister and a mother now to a role I had to adjust and settle into. I was now the caregiver and charged with seeing about everyone. So not only did my titles change, but now my focus and my desire to thrive in this role was now a priority.

THINGS HAD CERTAINLY CHANGED IN EACH SITUATION, AND TO THIS day I have adjusted accordingly. I believe I have done pretty well.

BE WILLING TO MAKE ADJUSTMENTS FOR THE TIMES IN YOUR LIFE WHEN there's a change. Don't be afraid. It's a step of faith that we must often take, if we are to stay in touch with the world. My challenge to each of you reading this is to embrace the newness and know that there is no right way nor wrong way to embrace change and make adjustments. You are challenged to do what is conducive for you.

Kimora Lee Simmons said, *"Life is a series of adjustments. You can make changes along the way, but if you don't start moving forward, you'll never get anywhere."*

Remember to *Adjust to Life's Circumstances*.

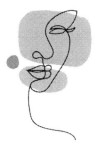

You are WOMAN!
W*hole-hearted;* ***W****ell-Balanced*
O*bservant;* ***O****pen-Hearted*
M*odest;* ***M****agical*
A*mazing;* ***A****dmirable*
N*urturing;* ***N****ice*

Date _____

Dear Me

_____
_____
_____
_____
_____
_____
_____
_____
_____
_____
_____
_____
_____
_____
_____
_____
_____
_____
_____

I Love You Always!

My Ideas & Inspiration

Chapter Fourteen

I AM RESILIENT, I AM WOMAN

Kimberly Babers

"I will praise thee, for I am fearfully and wonderfully made: marvelous are thy works..." (Psalms 139:14).

T he beauty and the fabric of a woman is a masterpiece to behold. The woman is God's glorious creation taken right out of the man. *"And the Lord God caused a deep sleep to fall upon Adam, and he slept; and he took out one of his ribs and closed the flesh thereof"* (Genesis 2:21). *"And the rib, which the Lord God had taken from man, made he a woman, and*

I AM RESILIENT, I AM WOMAN

brought her unto the man" (Genesis 2:22). *"And Adam said, this is now bone of my bone and flesh of my flesh: She shall be called woman, because she was taken out of man"* (Genesis 2:23).

THE ESSENCE OF A WOMAN IS INTRIGUING AND MYSTERIOUS simultaneously going beyond the surface level. What makes a woman intriguing? *"She is more precious than jewels, and nothing you desire can compare with her"* (Proverbs 31:10). Women have special features which makes them unique; they are nurturers, givers of life, and they flow in their femininity. *"Strength and honor are her clothing; and she shall rejoice in time to come"* (Proverbs 31:25).

WOMEN ARE PASSIONATE, STRONG, AND RESILIENT. SOMETIMES THE resiliency of women is the envy of some men. Women have the capability and fortitude to whether the storm and hold down their men helping, them to go through the storms of life with strength and tenacity. Biblical scripture describes the woman as the weaker vessel. *"Likewise, ye husbands, dwell with them according to knowledge, giving honor unto the weaker vessel...."* (1Peter 3:7). The woman being the weaker vessel is only related to the physical stature.

MANY TIMES, THE WOMAN IS THE GLUE THAT KEEPS THE FAMILY together and sets the tone and rhythm of the household. *"She looketh well to the ways of her household, and eateth not the bread of idleness"* (Proverbs 31:27). Women have an inner strength which regulates the heartbeat of many difficulties. Patience, perseverance, endurance, and resiliency are trademarks of strong women.

THE BIBLE HAS SHOWCASED MANY GREAT WOMEN OF FAITH, WISDOM, and strength. Some of those women include Ruth a Moabite woman who was loyal and showed kindness to her mother- in-law Naomi. Naomi became a widow when her husband and sons died. Ruth being a Moabite was converted and put her trust in God following the example of Naomi.

Ruth worked hard to provide for herself and Naomi in the midst of a famine.

Deborah was a prophet, and the only female judge in the Bible, she was a brave leader over Israel. She was very wise and courageous and led the people back to God, she put all her trust in God and carried out God's instructions. Lydia was a prosperous businesswoman who sold expensive purple cloths to make a living. Only wealthy people bought purple cloths. This was a great feat considering women in those days did not have businesses. Many biblical examples, exhibit the resiliency of women from generation to generation. Strength has been passed on to this generation of women who have faced adversity, setbacks and opposition which required strength beyond measure.

THROUGHOUT HISTORY WOMEN WERE VIEWED AS PROPERTY OR second-class citizens without rights or equality. Some women have suffered through disrespect, mental and physical abuse, and trauma, being undervalued, overworked, and under-appreciated. Women have always had to work harder and sacrifice more to fight for gender equality. Since the beginning of time women have fought for equality and their place in a male dominated society. Although, many times their voices were not heard, the very essence of a woman speaks louder than words.

RESILIENT WOMEN HAVE WATCHED THE STRENGTH OF THEIR grandmothers, mothers, sisters, aunts, nieces, and friends being put to the test, to overcome, tragedies, overwhelming losses, disappointments, and setbacks. In the toughest circumstances women have learned to be flexible, unyielding, compassionate, and caring despite the circumstance. They displayed the mental and physical toughness needed to endure and overcome adversity.

I CAN IDENTIFY WITH THE RESILIENT WOMAN, SHE IS ME. SHE IS A woman who can accept and live with her truths and take responsibility for the outcomes of her actions and decisions. She is confident in her abilities and is not afraid to stand up for herself and others to make a difference in the lives of her family and the people around her.

IT TAKES WILL POWER TO GO ON, EVEN IF THAT MEANS GOING ON alone. *"...we glory in tribulations also: knowing that tribulation worketh patience, and patience, experience; and experience hope"* (Romans 5:4-3). I am resilient, through the storm and the rain, I am woman. Being resilient means to endure and withstand many trials, tribulations, persecutions, disappointments, setbacks, and obstacles and being able to adapt to many difficulties. Sometimes difficulties stretch me like a rubber band ready to pop, just like that rubber band, I will snap back in place.

The ability to handle pressure and withstand adversity takes strength which, is beyond the natural. God's supernatural grace and endurance power gives us the power to stand. *"Many are the afflictions of the righteous: but the Lord delivereth him out of them all"* (Psalms 34:19). There is resiliency in being able press forward to overcome obstacles and adversity. *"I can do all things through Christ who strengthens me"* (Philippians 4:13).

RESILIENT WOMEN HAVE STRONG MINDS WHICH, SETS THEM APART from other people. They have the will power to never quit. The mental capacity of a person determines how strong they can deal with pressure and adversity. Resiliency is something that cannot be taught, it is the ability to overcome hardships, difficulties, and trauma by having a positive mind set and coping skills. *"And be not conformed to this world: but be ye transformed by the renewing of your mind, that ye may prove what is that good, and acceptable, and perfect will of God"* (Romans 12:22).

A resilient woman thrives in negative situations and comes out victorious in the mist of the storm. Resiliency leads to victory and cancels out the victim mentality. What is the leading cause of having a victim mentality? When life situations occur, and the outcome does not seem favorable overshadowing optimism, victory, success, and prosperity. Having a strong mind set, self-control, courage and an optimistic outlook are characteristics of an overcomer.

. . .

SOME OF THE INWARD TRAITS OF RESILIENT WOMEN ARE HAVING AN optimistic mindset and the will power to never quit. Having an optimistic mindset is the first step to having a successful outcome and the ability to win and overcome. *"For as a man thinketh in his heart, so is he"* (Proverbs 23:7). Whatever a person thinks in their mind is what they will become or what they will accomplish in life. What goes into the mind enters the heart.

THIS IS A GOOD REASON TO GET NEGATIVE PEOPLE OUT OF YOUR CIRCLE and out of your life. Sometimes the people around you will try to put fire on a negative situation to discourage an optimistic viewpoint about a situation. A resilient mindset opposes defeat and mediocracy. There have been numerous times when my back was against the wall and the odds were stacked against me. When my strength ran out God's strength took over. The life of Apostle Paul in the Bible is a great example of resiliency. The words he spoke are a powerful reminder of resilience and strength. *"Therefore, I take pleasure in infirmities, in reproaches, in necessities, in persecutions, in distress for Christ's sake: for when I am weak, then am I strong"* (2 Corinthians 12:10).

RESILIENT WOMEN ARE LED BY THE SPIRIT OF GOD AND NOT BY THEIR emotions. *"Casting down imaginations, and every high thing that exalteth itself against the knowledge of God and bringing into captivity every though to the obedience to Christ"* (2 Corinthians 10:5). Walking in the spirit of God, helps to put your emotions in subjection to the will of God. Stress and anxiety, affects the mind, body and soul and affects the spirit. Find balance to release negative energy. Praying, fasting, reading the Word of God, taking walks, listening to music, dancing, and exercising are great remedies to release stress and negative energy.

HAVING A HEALTHY OUTLET WILL HELP WITH SELF-REGULATION AND the ability to be calm in stressful times. It is a great idea to have a network of trusting people in your corner. It is important to talk someone about the different stressors in your life. A counselor, pastor, a good friend, or someone who can give you advice based on their life situation. It is important talk with someone who understands the struggles that you may face. It is always wise to seek Godly counsel from a pastor or a clergy leader, the wisdom of God is the beginning of understanding. *"A wise man will hear, and will increase learning, and a man of understanding shall attain unto wise counsels"* (Proverbs 1:5).

SECOND, PUSH THROUGH DIFFICULT OBSTACLES. PUSHING THROUGH tough situations and obstacles requires perseverance and the ability to keep going and not stop when facing a challenge or adversity. Many people quit and give up when the going gets tough. Standing when your strength is being tested builds character. It is not how you start the race but how you finish. *"...the race is not given to the swift or strong, but to those who endure to the end"* (Ecclesiastes 9:11).

OVERALL, IN SUMMARY THE CARES OF LIFE, THE HUSTLE AND BUSTLE and the management of everyday life can wear a good woman down. Challenges, tasks, and deadlines brings on pressure. When difficulties arise the best way to take them on is to have a mindset to win, accomplish and never give up. Having a mindset of Christ, wisdom, self-control, and a strategy are ways to conquer any difficult situation.

THE WORLD IS CHANGING SO RAPIDLY, IT WILL TAKE RESILIENCY IN the home, in the workplace, and for everyday living. Our very existence is being threatened by the atrocities being committed in this dispensation of time. The scriptures tell us, *"These things I have spoken unto you, that you might have peace. In this world ye shall have tribulation: but be of good cheer; I have overcome the world"* (John 16:33). Knowing that the Lord has paid the price for all the trials and tribulations which have occurred in our life makes life easier. Going through the storms of life will build our character and will continue to shape you into the resilient woman, you are today.

I AM WOMAN!

Wise
Overcomer
Motivated
Amazing
Never quit

Date _____

Dear Me

_____
_____
_____
_____
_____
_____
_____
_____
_____
_____
_____
_____
_____
_____
_____
_____
_____
_____

I Love You Always!

My Ideas & Inspiration

Chapter Fifteen

RESTORATION = PREPARATION + TIMING

Tracey Ellis-Carter

"Keep me as the apple of the eye, hide me under the shadow of thy wings." Psalm 17:8

January 3, 2015 (journal entry)

"Happy New Year! God loves me! I am God's Beloved! Yes, it's a new year and this year I have decided not to focus on a New Year's Resolution, but a New Life change - getting back to the basics - spiritually, physically, and financially. It is time for healing!"

WHO WOULD HAVE KNOWN THAT SHORTLY AFTER WRITING THIS journal entry I would experience a moment of trauma? How could the weight of darkness come and interrupt the excitement I hoped the new year would bring?

In that season I fell into a sunken place desperately trying to hold on to God's promise for my life. He promised that he would never leave me or forsake me. He promised that He would restore and replace all that I believed that I had lost with something far greater. I have always fought and conquered battles that have come my way, but nothing could have prepared me for what was happening. I was falling apart, emotionally, mentally, and physically. How could I find the strength to get through each day? God reminded me of His promise in Ephesians 6:10-12, "Be strong in the Lord and the power of his might. Put on the whole armor of God, that you may be able to stand against the wiles of the devil. For we wrestle not against flesh and blood but against principalities, against powers, against the rulers of the darkness of this age, against spiritual hosts of wickedness in heavenly places."

THIS LIFE CHANGING MOMENT HAD BECOME MY KRYPTONITE attempting to destroy me. I had always thought of myself as a warrior, but this battle was getting the best of me. My mind was spinning daily as I tried to understand what was going on, but no matter how much I thought about it, I couldn't make sense out of any of it. How could 23 years of marriage no longer matter? I had so many questions of why. Questions that neither of us could clearly answer and at that very moment, I remembered Proverbs 3:5-6 "Trust in Jehovah with all thy heart, and lean not upon thine own understanding" (American Standard Version). I can and should trust God. God has never failed me, He has always been my protector, my healer, and my peace. The journey was difficult and at times I had little to no faith that God would restore. I felt lost as though I had fallen into a dark abyss. I had to find a way out, I had to find "ME" - WHO AM I? I no longer felt safe, secure, confident, strong, and capable. I no longer saw ME. Looking in the mirror, I saw the brokenness. My brokenness distracted me from seeing that who I am is beautiful.

AT THE TIME, MY FAMILY AND I LIVED A GOOD LIFE ABROAD, BUT NOW we faced the decision to leave that life abroad somehow, that good life meant nothing as it all seemed to come to an end.

Choosing to return to the United States was difficult, leaving a place we considered "home" to try and save my marriage was frightening. So, I sold all that I could, packed my bags and took a flight to return to the United States. It was TIME to heal in a place where I could be loved on and feel safe spiritually, supported, encouraged, motivated, and recharge. I returned with a mission, to fight for my marriage and keep my family whole.

I REMEMBER A GIRLFRIEND TELLING ME - "TRACEY, LET HIM GO." I couldn't believe what she was saying. I thought as my friend she should be on my side. "Let him go?" I thought. How could she so boldly say this? After all, what did she know when she still had her husband, her family? Although her words stung, the truth was she was on my side. She cared enough to not want me to hurt any longer. I struggled to accept those words, but it was at that very moment that God spoke and reminded me that my husband IS NOT my God! You see, I worried a lot and constantly about myself about my husband at the time, about what he wanted, what he was thinking, and the choices he was making. Although I was praying, I continued to be consumed by the trauma within my marriage, giving God the bare minimum. If I was truly going to walk this faith walk, I had to let go to heal. An overnight quick fix would have been ideal and although healing has no time frame, God knew the work needed for me. Seven years have passed and I continue to put the work in - I am a work in progress!

. . .

FAST FORWARD, I STOPPED PLAYING GAMES AND COMMITTED TO LIVE each moment and the rest of my days with intent – My year of Full Restoration! In this season, I am where I belong!

I didn't do it alone. God blessed me with a village, a tribe I hold near and dear to my heart, they were food to my soul. They prayed with and for me, cried with me, laughed with me and gave me "real talk." Two of those people were my beautiful aunts who took the time to write me these beautiful letters and the other are words that God spoke clearly to me:

"Yes, you have had some calamity in your life, but I love you, I believe in you. Whatever you are going through is only a test and this too shall pass. I only wish I could be with you at this time in your life. Although I don't know the circumstances, listen girl I want you to remember that you are an EXTRAORDINARY woman, mother, wife, sister, and friend. I am proud of you, the things you've accomplished and the courageous way you have lived your life. Remember this, The Lord is your shepherd...you shall not want no matter how bleak it seems. Know this, wherever you are on this journey just start Praising God even when you can't see the "pot of gold" at the end of the rainbow you know God is working behind the scene and He is working it out for you. Praise Him for the past, the present and the unknown future – TRUST HIM"

-Auntie Shay

"YOU ARE SOMETHING, LIFE COMES ALONG AND TRIES TO KNOCK YOU down and what do you do? You rise. Not right away, not like some comic book character, but gracefully. Gathering strength as you go you rise. And you emerge stronger, more beautiful, more empowered than ever before...you amaze me you make me proud to be your auntie."

-Auntie Debra

COME MY BELOVED. My arms are wide open. I welcome you into my bosom. Feel my love engulf you as I am making you NEW. Release fully unto me all that burdens your soul for I am the lover of your soul. You are perfect for me. No imperfections I see only beauty, loveliness, purity of heart. My heart reaches out to yours to engulf the hurts that have plagued you. I am giving you a garment of praise for the spirit of heaviness. I am releasing unto you, pure joy. Grasp hold of the gifts I present to you my precious one.

-Love Daddy

I'm sharing hoping if "your world is crumbling" it's ok to cry those tears, it's ok to scream and seclude yourself for a moment to restore (Psalm 30:4-7). Gain the strength to get back up and know that your latter will be greater (Jeremiah 29:11). Look in your mirror and remind yourself that you are amazing, you are beautiful and you are the apple of his eye.

I thought what I had then was a big deal, but what is happening now far exceeds what I had. I love myself for who I see myself to be and not how others see me. I love myself for the woman I have become and I am beyond excited for my life past, present, and future.

I Am Woman

Wise
Observant
Magnificent
Astute
Nurturing

Date _____

Dear Me

_____
_____
_____
_____
_____
_____
_____
_____
_____
_____
_____
_____
_____
_____
_____
_____
_____
_____

I Love You Always!

My Ideas & Inspiration

Chapter Sixteen

WHAT I GLEANED FROM GLO

Lisa Middlebrooks

I n the beginning God created Man and called him Adam. He then created woman from Adam's rib and named her Eve. HE did so as state, "it's not good for Man to be alone, I will create a companion for him. (To paraphrase KJV BIBLE)

The word **Womanhood** can be defined per Merriam Webster's - Dictionary as:

A.) The state of being a woman. It further outlines: B.) distinguishing character or qualities of a woman or of woman kind.

. . .

THE WORDS ABOVE ARE WHAT I SAW DISPLAYED GROWING UP BY THE model I hold to be one who was the Epitome of Womanhood. My mother, Gloria Morgan.

MAMA WAS BORN DURING THE GREAT DEPRESSION NEAR THE TOBACCO farms in West Virginia. She was the eldest child of her parent's large brood. Which during that time that was perfectly normal to have large families. As the eldest, she would be relied upon to assist in the care of her younger siblings

Upon high school graduation she got married and left her parents' home and started her own family. Life challenges found her settling in a Midwestern city. It is where she relied on many traits that represented that of a WOMAN. As soon as her girls were ready, she extolled those lessons and values upon them. Gloria/Mama was always thought of as loving, kind, supportive of all those with which she was cared for and loved.

MAMA WAS WHAT MANY THOUGHT AND COMMUNICATED TO BE, A NATURAL beauty. She didn't like and rarely used make-up. The only exception was the POP of red lip. Which became her signature look. She NEVER went anywhere without it, right down to the corner store.

Growing up, I recall how much care Mama took with her appearance. As beautiful as she was, there were steps taken in preparation. An event, a typical workday, family gathering. In the early years, when funds were scarce, I watched her unselfishly go without many things she considered important to for beauty regiment/necessary items to insure her children had.... new clothes, shoes, lipstick, stockings. I mean she would wear shoes with obviously worn heels, stockings in disrepair, doing her own hair. Taking ALL resources and allocating extra to her children. Never once a complaint, cross word to any of us. We NEVER knew there were challenges economically. That is where her WIT came into play. If we didn't care for the dinner option.... she would respond, "well if you don't eat it that's fine, but before I make something else your stomach will be shaking hands with your back," then we didn't understand what that meant. As we became older it has become a family joke. Her **WIT** is what got us through those times.

THROUGH IT ALL SHE WAS ALWAYS **OPTIMISTIC**. SHE ALWAYS could see the light at the end of the tunnel. And encouraged me to adapt a "glass half full" way of thinking/believing. BE POSITIVE.

THE **MAJESTIC** VISUAL OF HER BEAUTY WAS THAT WHEN SHE entered a room the entire room would notice. She had the beauty that could stop a clock. Though others may think, believe, and offer compliments of your beauty, it is necessary to conduct yourself in a dignified fashion. Smile and nod, thanking others for noticing.

AGELESS IS ANOTHER ATTRIBUTE THAT CAN BE SEEN AS A characteristic of womanhood. My mother and her mother (my grandmother) were two of the most alluringly ageless women I have ever seen or known. I wish they bottled and sold their "secret" to the fountain of youth. It was often said or remarked that we all looked like "sisters" and they didn't look like my elders. Even unto their eventual demise. People were shocked when they realized their actual chronological ages. Their smooth skin, small frames, beautiful smiles and laughing eyes. All of which further demonstrates those characteristics of a woman.

NURTURER IS WHAT I FEEL IS ONE OF THE MOST IMPORTANT characteristics of being a WOMAN lending to the overall make up of womanhood. One of the most important characteristics of a woman is to be a nurturer. What needs to be understood is that while most mothers and caregivers are nurturers. It is not a "pre-requisite" for being a member of womanhood. To know and understand there is a balance between training a bird to fly using techniques and when the birdie is ready to fly alone.

. . .

HARDWORKING - A FEMALE WHO IS A GO-GETTER OR hardworking will formulate a plan and stick with it. She recognized to achieve what she wanted in life she MUST work long laborious hours. Sometimes with little or NO pay. She had a plan and would not give up or give in until the end. My mom went back to school after the final birdie graduated high school and left the nest. This resulted in her obtaining her BS degree and volunteering in a variety of ways. She became politically active. So much she was invited and attended President Clintons inaugural ball and received a personally signed thank you letter for her participation signed by President Clinton. This besides working Full-time.

OBSERVANT - THE ABILITY TO SURVEY THE LAND SO TO SPEAK AND never miss a beat. One must keep watch of all surrounding people places things. Read people, words, actions and such. To insure those that are close aren't in need of your assistance.

ORGANIZED - ENSURING THAT YOUR WORLD/LIFE IS ORGANIZED. She developed methodologies for keeping up with things. Developing a scheme to assist with working with records, money, household items, schedules. To ensure things are not lost or skipped

DEPENDABLE THE LAST CHARACTERISTIC WHEN ASSESSING A trait for each letter. That would involve a level of trust. This would be the level of reliability

THIS IS WHAT **WOMANHOOD** MEANS TO ME. FORTUNATELY, I HAD the opportunity to watch, listen, look and learn. From a WOMAN who took seriously what she showed her children and didn't think or realize we were watching and learning. Most of the time she just knew we were not and believed her efforts were all in vain. Gloria Morgan this is ALL for you and because of you. I not only owe you life but had a positive model that trained me on how to perform in the "world" of womanhood.

I was fortunate to have the BEST TEACHER EVER. This is What I Feel about Womanhood. And What I Actually Gleaned from GLO

WITTY
OBSERVANT
MAJESTIC
ALLURINGLY AGELESS
NUTURING
HARDWORKING
OPTIMISTIC
ORGANIZED
DEPENDABLE

Date _____

Dear Me

_____
_____
_____
_____
_____
_____
_____
_____
_____
_____
_____

_____
_____
_____
_____
_____
_____

I Love You Always!

My Ideas & Inspiration

Chapter Seventeen

LESSONS ALONG THE JOURNEY

Joyce Jennings

A s an infant your first bonding experience is with your mother and it continues to grow with nurture and care beyond the womb into adulthood. Yet, for many that is not the case, such as mine. Due to circumstances, I was reared in an environment of unhappiness. My father was absent and the one closest to me, my mother, was mentally afar from me.

How could it be one of frailty would one day have to experience life lessons and gain wisdom not from the one that birth them but all alone because in the mind of the one life was ended due to absence before life ever truly began?

Life lessons have taught me love and self-respect must come from within. You cannot allow other's thoughts and opinions be the guide and parameter of how you think of yourself. Happiness is a choice and one must choose daily whether they want to be governed by the day's events or by the energy they produce. I choose happiness!

I Am Woman...I choose to be positive and I know good things will happen to and for me!

I Am Woman...I have decided this is my time to shine! No longer will I allow how I grew up nor what happened in my past to define who I am!

Woman...no longer will I hold my head down awaiting approval from others! I am my biggest supporter and greatest cheerleader!

WOMAN... I KNOW MY WORTH! VALIDATION OF WHO YOU ARE IS NOT needed from anyone. Set your standards and expectations and do not compromise to accommodate anything or anyone that is against your belief.

WOMAN...I HAVE BEEN BROKEN BUT, ONLY GOD CAN HEAL AND MEND the areas of your life that needs His special touch. Do not believe that a man or anyone else for that matter can fix you. Special note: Only men who are broken themselves will say something like that. Two broken halves doesn't make a whole, it only makes a hot mess (shaking my head). I had to learn the hard way.

WOMAN...DAILY AFFIRM YOURSELF TO BE THE GREATEST! NO LONGER are you to just be alive, living in the state of existence with no or low self-esteem. No longer will I be a victim to verbal, emotional nor physical abuse. Intentionally, I will avoid negativity attracting negativity.

Lessons along this journey is truly life altering. A woman, in the sense of a mother in the black community is highly respected although, many are left to raise their children alone. But still single mothers you are celebrated because YOU are I Am Woman.

. . .

WOMAN...NOT ONLY DO YOU GIVE BIRTH TO A CHILD...YOU, NURTURE, teach, direct and influence not only your child but a nation. You must know and remember that you are important.

WOMAN...YOU MUST HAVE BALANCE NOT ONLY FOR YOU BUT FOR YOUR family. Allow yourself to receive love as well as give it. Yet, be mindful of who you give your love to; everyone is not deserving of your love.

WOMAN...IT IS ALWAYS BETTER TO BE REJECTED FOR SOMETHING THAT means you no good rather than accepted by something that will bring major detriment; meaning receive rejection as a sign of divine protection. It may not be the right situation for you.

I AM WOMAN...ENTITLEMENTS ARE HIDDEN EXPECTATIONS NOT AN appreciation. Nobody owes you anything out of life. Don't depend on others for financial support and validation because you might not get it. You are responsible for you and your happiness, not anyone else.

When people, both men and women let you know that you are not valued by them. Believe them the 1st time. People will show you by discarding your boundaries. Never try to prove them wrong by staying in a situation or with someone who doesn't value you. You will never change their mind about you.

I AM WOMAN...KNOW YOUR LIMITATIONS AND BOUNDARIES. DO NOT continue to entertain people that do not respect the boundaries that you have placed. There is nothing wrong with setting boundaries. There is nothing wrong with having limitations. What is wrong is you allowing others to disregard your feelings and your stance. For those who continue to ignore the set boundaries show them better than telling them...limit your contact and time spent with them. You cannot change people but you can change your interaction with them. Spend your valuable time with people who value you, not chasing people down that don't give a crap about you. That's called self-respect.

DURING THIS JOURNEY OF BECOMING A WOMAN I HAVE LEARNED MANY lessons but the most important is real simple: We all have a purpose in this life. No matter the circumstance or situation encountered you are important. Not all lessons experienced were happy go lucky as one may call them but, they shape and mold each of us to be the women that we are today. As we continue this journey as women always remember there is strength in the pain endured. There is joy in the tears you've cried. There is laughter in those lowly and lonely nights. There is love in the moments of hate. There is you, woman forever evolving, flourishing, rising, conquering, persisting, shining, restoring, creating, inspiring, empowering.

YOU...I Am Woman are here, here to stay...I can see you...I can hear you...I can feel you...

For just as you, I too...I AM WOMAN!

I AM WOMAN

Date _____

Dear Me

_____
_____
_____
_____
_____
_____
_____
_____
_____
_____
_____
_____
_____
_____
_____
_____
_____
_____
_____

I Love You Always!

My Ideas & Inspiration

WOMAN

Tracey Ellis-Carter

She rises to the greeting of mother Earth
Sun shining bright but she is the light
The light to this beautiful day
Planting both feet to the floor
She stands tall
She is ready, ready to walk in her purpose
Her destiny
Her stride is broad
Her head held high
Her mission - unstoppable
She is woman
The one that makes her man say, "Wo-man!"

Her hips are curved
Her shoulders are sleek
She does not waiver in her faith
Unstoppable is what she is
Pressing through with a force causing
many to seek her
wanting to be her
Many want to be IN her
And some seek to destroy her, crush her and make her think less of
herself
Yet, Her worth, yes her worth is more valuable than silver and gold her
worth is more precious than rubies
Her worth cannot be devalued
She is forever woman!

30 DAILY POSITIVE AFFIRMATIONS

1. I feel the love of others who are not around me.

2. I am an amazing gift to myself, my friends, and the world. I am too much of an amazing gift to feel self-pity.

3. I love and appreciate myself. I am who I am and I love myself.

4. I do not need the company of others to feel complete. I am more than enough. I enjoy being in my own solitude.

5. The past no longer matters. It has no control over me. What only matters is the present. What I do in the present will shape my future. The past has no say in this.

6. Everything that I need will be provided to me at the right time and the right place. When something is meant to happen it will happen.

7. It is too early to give up on my dreams. it is always too early to give up on my dreams.

8. I will not give up until I have tried everything. And when I have tried everything I will look for other ways to try.

9. I believe in myself and I believe in the path I have chosen. I cannot choose the obstacles in my way, but I can choose to continue on my path, because it leads to my goals.

10. I am not only enough, I am more than enough. I also get better every day I live. Tomorrow I will be a better version of myself than I was today.

11. I will not criticize myself. I will love myself for who I am and for what I have become.

12. I will award and praise myself for my accomplishments. I will not dwell on the praise of others for my own praise is more than enough.

13. I will not compare myself to anyone else because everyone is on their own personal journeys. My journey is unique and cannot be compared.

14. I will only compare myself to myself. I know what greatness I can accomplish and I will only hold myself to that.

15. I will not look at the darkness in the world around me but instead at the light that is within me.

16. I am happy with who I am. I am happy. I am in my own skin. I am enough and I do not need to be someone else.

17. The answer is always in front of me, even if I have not yet seen it. As long as I continued to search I will find the answer.

18. Every problem I ever face will have a solution. There has never been a question without an answer. I just need to discover the answer.

19. I am a smart, capable, brilliant woman, and I have everything I need to get through this. When I make it through this I will be better for it.

20. I am safe and I am well. I am healthy and I am loved.

21. I will follow my dreams no matter what happens around me. The only person who can prevent me from achieving my dreams is me.

22. Those who love me will always love me, even if they do not fully understand my dreams. True friends and family will love me regardless of what my dreams. False friends will love me because of my dreams.

23. I will accept people for who they are and will support them as they continue to follow their own dreams. Even if I do not understand I will always support them.

24. I will let go of my worries I cannot control. I will focus my energy on only what I can control.

25. I am fully in charge of my future. I am the only one who can dictate the outcome.

26. I fully trust my ability. I trust my ability to provide for my family. I trust in my ability to care for my family.

27. I will participate in the day to the greatest of my ability. I will give today my very best.

28. I wake up every morning with hope for the day. I will start my day out with joy as joy is what I want to give and what I want to receive.

29. Only my thoughts are my reality. I will focus on the good and the joyful and avoid the negative.

30. I will relax my mind and I will stop thinking of the false stories. I will allow my mind to unwind and be at peace.

RESOURCES FOR WOMEN

National Association of Women Sales Professionals
https://nawsp.org

Financial Women's Association
https://fwa.org

Association for Women in Science
https://www.awis.org/join/

Alliance for Women in Media
https://allwomeninmedia.org

Minority Business Development Agency
https://www.mbda.gov

National Association for Female Executives
https://www.nafe.com/join-today

Office of Women's Business Ownership
https://www.sba.gov/about-sba/sba-locations/headquarters-offices/office-womens-business-ownership

International Association of Women
https://www.iawomen.com

Business and Professional Women International
https://www.bpw-international.org

American Business Women's Association
https://www.abwa.org

National Suicide Prevention Line
800-273-8255
https://www.suicidepreventionlifeline.org

Depression Prevention Hotline
630-482-9696
https://www.spsamerica.org

Crisis Intervention Hopeline
919-231-4525
(Text at 1-877-235-4525)
https://www.hopeline-nc.org

National Sexual Assault Hotline
800-656-4673
https://www.rainn.org

National Eating Disorder Association
800-931-2237
https://www.nationaleatingdisorders.org

National Association of Anorexia and Eating Disorders
630-577-1330
https://www.anad.org

THANK YOU

Thank you for purchasing and reading this book, I Am Woman. I pray that every part of your life is filled with God's love, joy, peace, kindness and overflowing blessings.

I leave you with this special message from our Heavenly Father.

The words you are about to experience are true, for they come from the very heart of God. He loves YOU. And He is the Father you have been looking for all your life. This is His love letter to you.

My Beloved Daughter...

You may not know me, but I know everything about you.
Psalm 139:1
I know when you sit down and when you rise up.
Psalm 139:2
I am familiar with all your ways.
Psalm 139:3
Even the very hairs on your head are numbered.
Matthew 10:29-31
For you were made in my image.
Genesis 1:27
In me you live and move and have your being.

Acts 17:28
For you are my offspring.
Acts 17:28
I knew you even before you were conceived.
Jeremiah 1:4-5
I chose you when I planned creation.
Ephesians 1:11-12
You were not a mistake,
for all your days are written in my book.
Psalm 139:15-16
I determined the exact time of your birth
and where you would live.
Acts 17:26
You are fearfully and wonderfully made.
Psalm 139:14
I knit you together in your mother's womb.
Psalm 139:13
And brought you forth on the day you were born.
Psalm 71:6
I have been misrepresented by those who don't know me.
John 8:41-44
I am not distant and angry,
but am the complete expression of love.
1 John 4:16
And it is my desire to lavish my love on you.
1 John 3:1
Simply because you are my child and I am your Father.
1 John 3:1
I offer you more than your earthly father ever could.
Matthew 7:11
For I am the perfect father.
Matthew 5:48
Every good gift that you receive comes from my hand.
James 1:17
For I am your provider and I meet all your needs.
Matthew 6:31-33
My plan for your future has always been filled with hope.

Jeremiah 29:11
Because I love you with an everlasting love.
Jeremiah 31:3
My thoughts toward
you are countless as the sand on the seashore.
Psalm 139:17-18
And I rejoice over you with singing.
Zephaniah 3:17
I will never stop doing good to you.
Jeremiah 32:40
For you are my treasured possession.
Exodus 19:5
I desire to establish you with all my heart and all my soul.
Jeremiah 32:41
And I want to show you great and marvelous things.
Jeremiah 33:3
If you seek me with all your heart, you will find me.
Deuteronomy 4:29
Delight in me and I will give you the desires of your heart.
Psalm 37:4
For it is I who gave you those desires.
Philippians 2:13
I am able to do more for you than you could possibly imagine.
Ephesians 3:20
For I am your greatest encourager.
2 Thessalonians 2:16-17
I am also the Father who comforts you in all your troubles.
2 Corinthians 1:3-4
When you are brokenhearted, I am close to you.
Psalm 34:18
As a shepherd carries a lamb,
I have carried you close to my heart.
Isaiah 40:11
One day I will wipe away every tear from your eyes.
Revelation 21:3-4
And I'll take away all the pain you have suffered on this earth.
Revelation 21:3-4

I am your Father, and I love you even as I love my son, Jesus.
John 17:23
For in Jesus, my love for you is revealed.
John 17:26
He is the exact representation of my being.
Hebrews 1:3
He came to demonstrate that I am for you, not against you.
Romans 8:31
And to tell you that I am not counting your sins.
2 Corinthians 5:18-19
Jesus died so that you and I could be reconciled.
2 Corinthians 5:18-19
His death was the ultimate expression of my love for you.
1 John 4:10
I gave up everything I loved that I might gain your love.
Romans 8:31-32
If you receive the gift of my son Jesus, you receive me.
1 John 2:23
And nothing will ever separate you from my love again.
Romans 8:38-39
Come home and I'll throw
the biggest party heaven has ever seen.
Luke 15:7
I have always been Father, and will always be Father.
Ephesians 3:14-15
My question is...Will you be my child?
John 1:12-13
I am waiting for you.
Luke 15:11-32

Love, Your Dad.
Almighty God

MEET THE AUTHORS

I AM WOMAN

VERLISA WEARING

Visionary Author

Verlisa Wearing tenderly known as Elder V is a United States Marine Corp Veteran; Ordained Minister; CEO/Founder of It Is Written Publishing, LLC and The RiseHer Network, Multi-Bestselling Author and State Supervisor of KCFI-State of Georgia.

Verlisa established her businesses to help others shatter glass ceilings that are holding them captive not allowing their voices to be heard.

She helps aspiring, emerging and published authors, personal and professional development coaches write $aleable books in order to share their voice as experts and increase visibility and profitability.

Verlisa is committed to the empowerment of women from all walks of life. She is determined to help women find their voice and make their voice count.

She believes in order to see change; you first must focus on and create change within yourself so that you may help bring change in others.

When asked how she handles struggles of life she states, "*in every storm the sun must shine. If we just get through this, we will be stronger and wiser than ever. There will be brighter days.*"

When asked what she feels is her greatest accomplishment, she simply states, being the mommy of David, Daylon and Cai.

Her motto is *"Live a life that outlives you!"*

You may connect with Verlisa Wearing at the following media outlets:
Website: www.verlisawearing.com
Email: verlisa.wearing@therisehernetwork.com

facebook.com/verlisa.wearing

twitter.com/iamverlisa

instagram.com/verlisawearing

linkedin.com/in/verlisa-wearing-5b1924b6

DR. MONIQUE LATRICE

Break Free And Rise

Monique LaTrice is a writer, literacy advocate, and higher education professional. She earned a B.A. in English Literature, an M.A. in Communications, and her Ph.D. Dubbed the Age Affirmative Ambassador, Monique is creator and chief writer of **age·less** mindset blog, where she writes musings of encouragement and inspiration for women 40+ and she is featured in Author BAE magazine. Monique is an avid reader who enjoys traveling, and writing.

Monique is the author of the mini devotional *8 Weeks of Self Discovery* published in 2018, and the personal narrative, *Late Discovery* published in 2021. She is also a three times best-selling co-author of the anthologies: *Speak Up...We Deserve to Be Heard,* published in 2021, *Kept Promises: Prospering in a Pandemic*, published in 2021, and *Dear Young Woman volume 3: His Purpose is Greater Than Your Plan,* published in 2021.

You may connect with Dr. Monique LaTrice on the following media sites:

https://moniquelatrice.com
https://www.authorbaemagazine.com/post/featuring-dr-monique-latrice
https://risehermedia.com/dr-monique-latrice

facebook.com/dr.moniquelatrice
instagram.com/dr.moniquelatrice

DR. SHIRLEY BOYKINS BRYANT

I AM WOMAN

Dr. Shirley Boykins Bryant hails from Beaumont Texas. She is an Author, Behavioral Coach, and CEO of " Let's Talk About It LLC" and Educating our Youth, which is a non-profit.

Dr. Bryant has a Doctorate in Human and Organizational Psychology; she is a certified Emotional Intelligence and Cognitive Behavior Practitioner and has a Diploma in .Modern Applied Psychology.

She has written and published research titled "The Lived Experience HR Professionals during the COVID -19 Pandemic and Co-Authored God-Fident, an Anthology.

Dr. Bryant was featured in the Up Words Magazine, March 2022 edition for an article she wrote titled "A Women of Excellence".

Dr. Bryant is a veteran of the U.S. Army, she retired at the rank of SGM after serving honorably for 23 years..

Dr. Bryant's hobbies include spending time with her family, reading and traveling.

You may connect with Dr. Shirley Boykins-Bryant at the following media outlets:

f facebook.com/shirley.bryant.14

TANYA L. HOLLAND

I Woke Up Like This

Author Tanya L Holland resides in the Bronx, New York. She is the mother of six children and the grandmother of three. Her debut book, "Shirley Goodness & Mercy, (Living After My Mom No Longer Did)" has received rave reviews and 4/4 stars on the Online Book Club. It is due to be the "Book of the Day" on July 22nd of this year. She has since been part of two Amazon Bestsellers "Finding Joy In the Journey, Part 2" and "Dear Daughter Anthology."

She is a motivator who empowers women. She runs a Women's Support Group called "Motherless Daughters" which focuses on grief after the loss of mothers and other loved ones.

You may connect with Tanya L. Holland at the following media sites:
Website: www.Hollandwrites.com

facebook.com/hollandwrites
twitter.com/juicytatzi
instagram.com/juicytatzi

ZANETTA HOWARD

I Was Called To Be Hurt

Zanetta Howard is a woman of varied talents and accomplishments. She is known for her faith, determination, work with youth and young adults and most importantly as a woman of God. She is the wife of Darrell L Howard, mother of four adult children from previous marriage Tiara, Rodney, Jr. Devonne and Contessa, grandmother of (9). Daughter of Lawrence Zanders and Rev. Shirley Swain.

Formative education: Akron Public School System, Hammel Business College, Malone College, AIU University, Progressive Bible College and Multiple Nan McKay University and Jamie Kinney Consulting.

Zanetta has worked in the Housing Industry over 30 years, and currently serves as International Director of Women's Outreach and Communication Kingdom Connection Fellowship International, Dr. Bishop Yvonne Jones, Bishop of Women and Bishop Jerome H. Ross, Presiding Prelate.

Zanetta Marie is the host of *Keepin it Real Shock Talk*, Author with It Is Written Publishing and Sales Director and Anchor on The RiseHer Network!

You may connect with Zanetta Howard at the following media sites:
Email: zanetta.marie@theriseHernetwork.com

facebook.com/zmmcnab

twitter.com/PastorZee

instagram.com/zanetta_howard

linkedin.com/in/zanetta-howard-b578279

SANDRA E. JACKSON

You Are Fully Equipped To Survive

Born to the parents of Bishop Samuel I. Rumph and Elect Lady Priscilla M. Rumph, Sandra is the twelfth child. She is the CEO of Journey Into Purpose, LLC and a licensed Evangelist in the PCAFI organization.

As a shiftologist, Sandra E. Jackson empowers and shifts men and women from where they are right now to where God desires them to be. She is the mother of nine beauties, five daughters and four sons. She survived a divorce after being married for 20 years.

She acquired her Bachelor's degree in Biblical Studies and Minister in May 2020, during the pandemic from Nazarene Bible College in Colorado.

Sandra dreamt about hosting Sandra's Author's Forum Talk Show, which came to fruition in 2020. She interviews authors, entrepreneurs, businessmen, and women for one hour on radio and tv. In addition, she hosts a Marriage Symposium and interviews married couples letting the world know that marriages can survive during this season and a pandemic. Sandra is the author of #1 Amazon Best Seller *Trauma, Grief, Pain-bodies, & Healing* and coauthor of 6 books. Her newest project is the visionary of a fantastic anthology of 20 coauthors entitled *Life After...*

Her mission is: *If she can help somebody along the way, her life will not be in vain.*

Her favorite quote is: *I Am Ecstatic To Be Alive.*

You may connect with Sandra E. Jackson at the following media outlets:
Website: sandrarumph.com
Email: journeyintopurpose22@gmail.com

facebook.com/sandrasauthorforum

CHRISTINE JAMES

Worthy OF M.E.

Christine James of Chosen Minded LLC is a Confidence Coach & Strategist, Speaker and Author. She equips budding coaches, speakers, and trainers to develop a job exit strategy while packaging and pricing their brilliance for profit. She loves working with amazing women that know God has called & chosen them to make a greater impact now.

Christine has BS and is a certified Coach, Speaker and Trainer.

She is passionate about marriage, motherhood, mindset, entrepreneurship and seeing other women and men succeed beyond measure.

You may connect with Christine James at the following media outlets:

Website: https://www.christinemjames.com

facebook.com/chosen.minded.3

instagram.com/chosenminded

linkedin.com/in/christine-james-chosen-minded-coaching

SHAYLA UNIK

Lusting With Love

Shayla Unik Davis born and raised in Detroit, MI. and passionate about the importance of self-development. Life has presented many challenges. 2012, being a single mom and wanting to provide better, she moved back to Alabama hoping to start a new life. Through a few dead-end jobs, experiencing homelessness, a failed marriage, and a newborn, she decided to move back to Detroit determined to be a great mom, she knew things would get better.

2014 Shayla's HR career began. 2019 Shalya became an HR Certified professional through the Society of Human Resource Management (SHRM), holding an internationally recognized credential in HR and becoming HR Director earned her first publicized award from Michigan's Corp! Magazine as one of Michigan's Most Valuable Millennials for her hard work, dedication and contribution to HR. Nominated for Crain's 40 under 40 and accepted into Crain's Leadership Academy; Cohort 5.

April 2019, Shayla launched *Unik I Am* to support and uplift young ladies and women. Reminding them not to allow bad decisions/mistakes define nor confine them. She's sharing her story of going from homeless to HR Director, selling brand accessories. providing HR support to small businesses, and resume support. Shayla has presented as a guest at women empowerment events and vendor events. *"Because...everyone has a story, but your story is what makes you Unik"*.

You may connect with Shayla Unik at the following media outlets:
Website: www.unikiam.com
Email: shaylaunik@unikiam.com

facebook.com/UnikIAm2
instagram.com/unik_i_am2

DEBORAH JUNIPER-FRYE

The Evolved Woman

As a longtime Grief Specialist, Deborah Juniper-Frye has worked with countless families, individuals, and organizations through the grief process.

She is the Business Owner of Grief Care Consulting LLC; a Grief Recovery Method Specialist with 23 Years of Grief Experience and Expertise; Life & Recovery Coach; the Author of nine books, to include, Amazon Best Selling Author 7X's; Amazon International Best Selling Author; Global Conference Speaker; and a Contributing Writer for OWN IT Magazine.

Deborah has lived abroad as a military wife, resides in Virginia Beach, VA and has been madly in love with her husband, Michael for over 36 years. They have three adult children - Antione, Michael, Jr., and Whitney, as well as, three grandchildren, Antione, Jr., Aaliyah, and Raevyn.

You may connect with Deborah Juniper-Frye at the following media outlets:
Website: www.griefcareconsulting.com
Email: dfrye.gcc@gmail.com

facebook.com/deborah.frye.5

twitter.com/GriefCConsult

linkedin.com/in/deborah-frye-282732164

instagram.com/griefcareconsulting

DR. JENNOA GRAHAM

Single Parenting While in School - Best Practices

Dr. Jennoa R. Graham, aka Dr. GNP was born a Hoosier in Indianapolis, Indiana, and currently resides in the North Georgia area. Her experience as a young and impoverished single mother made her realize the value of hard work and building a better future for her son. This event was the catalyst in shaping her foundational love for finance, community, and servant leadership.

Now as a catalyst for others, Dr. GNP is an entrepreneur and holds several degrees, including a dual doctorate. She is an international public speaker, author, professor, executive team leader, and an occasional trumpet player.

Her 20-year career of combined multinational corporate accounting and consulting experience reflects core values of transparency, integrity, efficiency, and sustainability resulting in multi-million-dollar savings. As an active leader of Heavens Harvest Ministries, she facilitates workshops based on financial need, debt management, and life management.

You may connect with Dr. Jennoa Graham at the following media outlets:

facebook.com/jennoa.graham

linkedin.com/in/jennoagrahamphd

COLLEEN WILLIAMS-RENNIE

Time To Take A Stand

Born and raised in the beautiful Islands of Trinidad and Tobago; Colleen Williams always had a passion for writing poetry and short stories.

Her two releases *Stop* and *Blinded By Love* (both can be found on amazon.com) was written out of the painful experiences she had to endure in her life.

Coming from a rough past, it was hard for her to trust and forgive again, after years of abuse.

Colleen has done numerous interviews, and has been featured in a few magazines worldwide sharing her testimony about how she went from *Bitter and Broken to Beautiful and Blessed*.

She has inspired many women to walk away from abusive relationships and to know their worth. She continues fighting for women in domestic violence situations. She travels to prisons and battered women's shelter speaking to men and women letting them know if she can make it out so can they.

She now lives in Boston, Mass. When she is not writing she loves reading, traveling and teaching soccer.

You may connect with Colleen Williams-Rennie at the following media outlets:

Email: Empresscolleen617@gmail.com

facebook.com/colleenwilliams
twitter.com/Empresscolleen1

FRANCINE HOUSTON

Touching The Hem Of Jesus' Garment

Francine Houston is a multitalented individual who enjoys fashion, graphics/media and writing. She is a graduate of the College for Creative Studies in Detroit, Mich., with a bachelor's degree in communication design. Francine also earned associate's degrees in applied graphic design from Mott Community College in Flint, Mich., and in fashion design from the International Academy of Design and Technology in Troy, Mich. Furthermore, she is a graduate of the School of the Bible 2 in Southfield, Mich.

She is also the founder of two businesses: FH Designs, for which she is the principal fashion designer, and Cineik Media. Francine was recognized for her accomplishments with the Excellence Award from Women of Distinction magazine in 2015.

Francine is also a member of Lupus Detroit and helps with their events as much as possible. A lupus survivor, she wrote a book about her battle with the disease entitled *Lupus Journey*, published in 2016. Its sequel, *Life After Lupus*, was released in 2018. She was featured in Lupus Now magazine's Fall 2014 issue and graced the October 2018 cover of the periodical Discovering You. Her third book is *Strength of a Woman: The Last Journey*, a poetry and short-story book.Later this year, she recently published a self-care guide called *Everyday Heroes: Learning to Cope and Heal* (It's ok to take the cape off sometimes).

You may connect with Francine Houston at the following media outlets:

f facebook.com/francine.houston.52
🐦 twitter.com/HoustonFrancine
📷 instagram.com/francine.l.houston

BELINDA STROTHER

Who Do You Think You Are?

Belinda Strother is a 55-year-old woman from Boston. She retired from teaching English overseas to spend more time with family and friends. Upon returning home and dealing with a Worldwide pandemic, Belinda found her niche in creating unique crystal jewelry, writing and creating a life coaching program. She developed a new love of slime making which led to the development of her Etsy shop entitled Slime Concoctions. This way she can share her love of art and creating ways for adults to laugh and be lighthearted. She endeavors to be an integral part in helping adults to dream, smile, laugh and play their way to feeling healthy and whole. Additionally,

Belinda has been able to fulfill her desire to be a writer by contributing to 3 anthologies and is in the process of completing a 4th scheduled to be published the end of summer 2022.

You may connect with Belinda Strother at the following media outlets:
Email - pink4wellness53@gmail.com
Website - pink4wellnessbybelinda.com
Etsy Shop - slimeconcoctions.etsy.com

instagram.com/pink4wellness2
tiktok.com/@waistbeadsnintentions
facebook.com/Pink4wellnessbyBelinda

DR. ANITA GREEN

Adjusting To Life Circumstances

Rev. Dr. Anita Green, a native of Baltimore, Maryland, is a graduate of The University of Baltimore with a Bachelor of Arts degree in English Literature. She is a May 2009 graduate of the Morehouse School of Religion at the Interdenominational Theological Center (ITC), Atlanta, Ga. with a Masters of Divinity degree with a concentration in The Psychology of Religion and Pastoral Care. She is also a member of Theta Phi Honor Society.

In May, 2015, Rev. Green received her Doctor of Ministry degree from the ITC. Her Dissertation is titled – *"The Mourning After: How a Model of Aftercare Support Assists in the Healing Process of African American Women Experiencing Grief."*

Dr. Green is the CEO of The Grief Circle, a grief consulting firm, which partners with local funeral homes to provide grief support services and training to individuals, families, churches, organizations and funeral home staff.

She is a Certified Grief Coach and Grief Support Specialist.

She was inducted in the prestigious Martin Luther King Jr. Collegium of Scholars of Morehouse College, in March, 2017. She also serves as the National Alumni President of ITC, Chaplain of The Women of Distinction, Incorporated, Secretary of the Cobb County Chapter of The SCLC, Zeta Phi Beta Sorority, Incorporated and a member of The National Coalition of 100 Black Women Decatur/Dekalb Chapter.

Along with serving as the Chairperson of the Professional Advisory

Group for Chaplaincy at Grady Memorial Hospital in Atlanta, she is also an Adjunct Professor at Beulah Heights University and The Interdenominational Theological Center.

She currently serves as Associate Pastor and Congregational Care Servant Leader at Paradise Baptist Church in Atlanta, Ga.

facebook.com/anita.green.798

instagram.com/revdr.anitagreen

KIMBERLY BABERS

I Am Resilient, I Am Woman

Evangelist Kimberly Babers is a native of Pennsylvania and a current resident of Georgia. She has two children and four grandchildren. She believes in the empowerment of people through the Word of God, and the power of prayer and intercession.

Ms. Babers is an educator, mentor, and a spiritual covering for the youth she has instructed. She has made an impact in the lives of over 3,000 youth from various parts of Georgia helping them to overcome obstacles and reclaim their lives. She is a retired United States Army service member. She has traveled to many stateside locations, and various overseas locations which, include Germany, Korea, Hawaii, Guam, Egypt, Saudi Arabia, and Iraq.

Ms. Babers educational background includes a Master of Arts in Education with a concentration in Special Education from Grand Canyon University (GCU). She holds both a Bachelor of Arts and a Master of Arts degree in Transportation and Logistics Management from American Military University (AMU).

TRACEY ELLIS-CARTER

Restoration=Preparation+Timing

Tracey Ellis-Carter is a passionate educator with over 25 years' experience. She holds undergraduate and graduate degrees in Education and Reading & Literacy, respectively. She began her teaching journey in her hometown, Detroit. Later, she relocated to the Atlanta area where she continued her passion to educate our youth.

Tracey's prowess and passion led her abroad to the United Arab Emirates where she continued to extend her teaching abilities and became a mentor to other teachers as the Head of Faculty. She later returned to the Atlanta area, where she currently resides, to be closer to family and continue her pursuit of excellence at the same school she was once named *Teacher of the Year*.

Today, she extends her passion by offering tutoring and financial literacy services through her company, Milestones Educational Consulting and Tutoring

She is mom to four great children, and enjoys traveling, poetry, and all things music.

You may connect with Tracey Ellis-Carter at the following media outlets:
email: tracey.carter87@gmail.com
Milestones Educational consulting and Tutoring: https://www. milestonesconsulting.org/
UCES financial Advocate: www.ucesprotectionplan.com/TCarter57

facebook.com/tracey.elliscarter

twitter.com/kelaki4

instagram.com/traceyccarter

LISA MIDDLEBROOKS

What Gleaned From Glo

Lisa Middlebrooks is an established author with a a heart to help those that are less fortunate and those struggling to find their way.

Her Mantra.....*NEVER LOSE .HOPE!!* She understands how it feels to not be valued or considered and she makes every effort to give an arm or hand to her fellow Sister.

You may connect with Lisa Middlebrooks at the following media outlet:

 facebook.com/lisa.middlebrooks

JOYCE JENNINGS

Lessons Along The Journey

Born and raised in Chicago, Illinois, Joyce Jennings is a US Navy Veteran, Established Author, Community-oriented Leader, and Advocate who serves as an embodiment of vitality to many. Joyce is an alumnus of the Chicago Public Schools. She attended Northern Illinois University and graduated from DeVry Institute, Chicago with a Bachelor's degree in Computer Information Systems. Joyce has fourteen years of exceptional experience serving her country in the US Navy Reserves. During this time, she was deployed to serve in several places and countries, including Iraq.

Joyce is an Activist who strongly believes in standing up for the rights of people. She is mostly inspired by the saying, *"I'm no longer a victim but a survivor. I'm breaking those chains of poverty, codependency, shame, and worthlessness by telling my story. I am an unapologetic Black woman."*

Playing a vital role as an advocate, she has participated in several of the Black Lives Matter protests. Joyce is an active member of the National Organization for Women and the NAACP. As someone who enjoys giving back to the community, she is a proud member of Zeta Phi Beta Sorority, Inc.

Aside from her many accomplishments in community services, Joyce is also a Writer and she published her 1st book, *"Bad Company Damages Spiritual Growth."* In this personal and instructional book, Joyce guides people in identifying toxic people in their lives and provides ways to deal with them. She is also a contributing author for several books.

You may connect with Joyce Jennings at the following media outlet:

f facebook.com/Zetadiva4

ACKNOWLEDGMENTS

So grateful to *Dr. Monique LaTrice; Dr. Jennoa Graham*; *Dr. Shirley Boykins-Bryant*; *Dr. Anita Green*; *Zanetta Howard*; *Deborah Juniper-Frye*; *Kimberly Babers; Colleen Williams-Rennie; Francine Houston; Belinda Strother, Tanya L. Holland; Sandra E. Jackson; Joyce Jennings; Tracy Ellis-Carter* and *Lisa Middlebrooks* for believing in my vision for this book. Each of you embodied the very essence of my heart as you shared your stories.

Thankful for the gift of my mother, *Vera Johnson*-your confidence in me and the woman I am becoming causes me to be in awe. You are and have always been my greatest cheerleader! As you always say to me, I can do anything that I put my mind to do...show up and be great.

Grateful to my daughter, *Cai* who effortlessly remind me of the innocence of little girls and the feeling of joy to be a part of their growing into beautiful young ladies. You continue to encourage me to show up for my life especially when I do not want to.

And to my ride or die, my sons, *David* and *Daylon*, who I once held in my arms who are now champions me in all that I do and desire to do-thank you for being my inspiration and motivator.

NOTES

Campbell, Gordon. The Holy Bible: King James Version, Quatercentenary Edition. Oxford: Oxford University Press, 2010. https://www.amazon.com/dp/0199557608/ref=rdr_ext_tmb

1. Wikipedia

2. https://dictionary.cambridge.org/us/dictionary/english/adjustment

I AM WOMAN EXTRA!

You've made it, I am so proud of you, Sis! Did you gain some nuggets of wisdom? Have you written your Dear Me letter reminding yourself, you can do anything you desire? Did you write out your list of inspirations; have you accomplished any? Share with me. I want to support you every step of your journey in becoming the greatest first version of yourself. Let's communicate, tell me how you're doing and the steps you're taking. Send me an email at verlisa.wearing@ therisehernetwork.com, I promise to respond.

Do you want to be a part of a genuine sisterhood that fosters the success of our sisters around the world, one story at a time with one voice?

Be a part and join us at https://www.facebook.com/IAMWOMANRISEHER.

Do you have something to say? Are you ready to share your story? Contact *It Is Written Publishing, LLC* today for your self-publishing needs.

www.itiswrittenpublishing.net

Join the I AM WOMAN movement by registering for the upcoming I AM

WOMAN Summit, September 28th - September 30th, 2022. Register for this amazing Hybrid Conference at https://iamwomansummit.com/register-for-free

I AM WOMAN

Made in the USA
Middletown, DE
17 January 2023

21632141R00137